MOCHA

Chocolate

M O C H A

Edited by
Shani Greene-Dowdell
Published by
Nayberry Publications
www.nayberrypublications.com

Chocolate

Published by Nayberry Publications | 334-787-0733
www.nayberrypublications.com | info@nayberrypublications.com

Edited by Shani Greene-Dowdell | editing@nayberrypublications.com

ISBN: 978-0981584348
LCCN: 2010907149

Cover Design: Nayberry Publications.

Nayberry Publications World Wide website address is www.nayberrypublications.com

Printed in the USA

Hi Reader!

Thanks for making it possible for the second in the Mocha Chocolate Series to be released. Without your support, we could not continue to make this happen.

So, there will be no fluffy talk or long list of acknowledgements and dedications this time.

Turn the page.

This one is hotter than summer in Alabama!

Love ya,
~Shani

Table of Contents

Babygirl Strikes Back
Part I

by

Shani Greene-Dowdell

Sitting in my four-cornered room, the walls seemed to be closing in on me. The vibes from Minnie Riperson's *Memory Lane* coming through my radio reminded me of a harsh reality. The harsh reality that the man that I once thought was the "love-of-my-life" was gone, and this time, for good. As much as I hated to admit it, I had to come to grips with the fact that he was out of my life with no possibility of return. The warmth of Jack Daniels could not comfort my lonely and cold heart.

Truth be told, since Damon left, I had all but given up on men completely. For one solid year, I hadn't so much as felt the warmth from the touch of a man. More to that, I had not even had a meaningful conversation with the opposite sex. As far as I was concerned, men were the enemy. Their companionship was meaningless!

I somberly walked over to my CD case and turned the depressing memory-provoking melody off. Frequent trips down memory lane were not all they were chocked up to be. I'd had had one flash back to the past too many.

As much as I wanted to continue to sit around and sulk about Damon, I knew it was time to incorporate a part of my life that I'd come to considered a forbidden fruit. Men. The dirty M-word was becoming more and more essential to my wellbeing as the days passed by.

It was time for me to at least go to a place where I could steal wanting gazes at some of the sexiest men on the planet. I made my way over to my dresser to look for a comb to do something with my disheveled hair. I had not even so much as curled my hair in weeks, much less wrapped it at night. Scrunchies and ponytails had become my best friends. Once I released my hair from the hair bow to comb it, the sight in the mirror shocked me. I knew letting my hair go like I had done was just a shame and a sin against fashion.

"I have to get myself together," I spoke somberly to the image in the mirror as I picked up my pink comb and brush set and separated them placing the brush back on the dresser. I took the comb and started to stroke my long hair. A voice deep within me started to speak, but I quieted it with thoughts of my meeting at work where I was going to have to compete with Kenzie Yancey for ideas for the new minority finance initiative at work. I was definitely more qualified and dedicated to the cause than Kenya, but she had a way of flaunting around and kissing up to the powers that be. As soon as the thought of that dreaded meeting dissipated, my alter ego, Babygirl, spoke up interrupting a treasured moment of internal silence.

"*Stop whimpering around over some punk who has gone on and forgot about the both of us,*" she chastised me in a stern voice. "*It's not like he's the only man in town, girl. Pull your self together, get dressed, and let's go get our groove back tonight!*"

With a years worth of celibacy under my belt, not only was I deprived of some of the most beautiful moments love and lust has to offer, but my alter ego, Babygirl, was becoming harder and harder to live with. She was begging for a comeback of sexual satisfaction. I had done well to keep her suppressed for an entire year.

I looked around my bedroom in shock because her voice was startling. Babygirl hadn't formulated any words since Damon left. I guess I had successfully kept her quiet for as long as I could, but my promiscuous female organ was officially off hiatus and ready to take charge of my body.

"Don't stand there acting like you're surprised to hear from me. I let you go on long enough with this Damon drama, but it's Saturday night, a year to the date that he left us, and it's a perfect night for a one-night stand with a lucky chap at the local nightclub. Let's do it."

"I don't know about all of that," I told her sounding like a child being scolded by her mother. "I'm not up for meeting a stranger and running off to some cheap motel with him. That is what got me into the situation I was in with Damon. Disrespected, left alone, and hurt. Let me handle this Babygirl. You just sit back and relax and I will find us a respectable relationship to get involved with."

"See that is your problem. We are not looking for a man for you to marry tonight, just someone that can put out my flame. Don't you want to feel the powerful eruption that can come from sexy man's tool sliding inside of your warm body?"

I smiled thinking about the last time I made love and how intense it had been. I really did need to feel a man, if only just for tonight. Before I could realize it, I had fallen lock-in-step in with Babygirl's hypnotic voice. Intuitively, I walked over to my walk-in closet to find something sexy to wear. I selected a form-fitting black dress and diamond studded black stilettos.

"Uh, uhh...We can get sexier than that," Babygirl commanded. I should have told you that she could be so bossy. She was half of the reason I always ended up in man trouble because instead of thinking with my head I followed wherever she led me.

Placing the black dress back on the hanger, I rolled my eyes and continued to thumb through the various items in my closet to find something sexy, but not slutty.

"Wear the pussycat suit, so they can see what I'm working with," she hyped me up to wear a skintight cat suit number that I had not sported in years. To my surprise, I was all for it.

I might not have had sex for the past year, but I had definitely been hitting the gym to work off my frustration. I also had not been eating much because of the grief of losing Damon. To say the least, my body was fit and primed for the sexy cat suit, so I wanted to show off my newfound figure. I pulled the cat suit down and marveled over it.

"You know, if I wear this, we are going to shut the club down, Babygirl," I said, truly excited to be in good spirits for a change. Just the thought of wearing a sexy outfit and going to the club had me juiced.

"My intentions, exactly. I've waited a year for you to stop mourning Damon and move on to something bigger and better, and I do mean bigger and better! Tonight, we're officially getting back in the game. Remember how I used to tremble when I was at the epitome of pleasure. Remember wave after orgasmic wave with a fine specimen to share it with. Remember that Sasha? I want that, tonight."

"No, we need that tonight," I chimed in. Babygirl was so full of lustful passion that I had completely fallen under her spell. I briefly considered laying on the bed to please her until we both fell into post masturbation euphoric sleep, but I decided against it. If I did end up some man's sex vixen for the night, I wanted to be hypersensitive with each sensation moving through me like a new tidal wave.

To work myself up, I turned the radio back on and Gerald Levert's *Made Love to Ya* was playing. His songs had a way of driving me to the brink of sensuality, so I let that play at a nice and soft volume as I readied myself for a long night.

For a fleeting moment, I thought about ditching the thought of going out and staying at home stowed away from any trace of men. I logged onto my computer to distract myself from my thoughts and low and behold the first advertisement I saw on the computer was a Trojan bullet commercial. Some woman was on there talking about how the bullet kept her satisfied all day, even at work, until she was able to get home to make love to her husband.

Dang, I've got to order me one of those, I thought as I quickly powered my computer off.

Just that fast I had gotten caught up in another sexual fantasy. It would be nice to have a Trojan bullet to use all day and a husband at home waiting for me after a long day at the bank. Whew! Was everything about sex these days?

It seemed that I was a good girl living in a sexual world, but Babygirl was doing everything in her power to convert me over to the bad side. I knew that with her in her current state of sexual frustration there would be no way that I could quench her hunger by mechanical means tonight. Therefore, one hour later I was dressed in my black cat suit, diamond-studded stilettos, and standing in front of critically-acclaimed night spot, Pleasure Castle.

Pleasure Castle was a dual women's and men's strip club where some of the sexiest strippers and patrons on this side of Alabama intermingled. Often times, couples came to Pleasure Castle to get roused up enough to go home and fulfill their most mind-blowing sexual fantasies with each other.

"Yeah baby, thank you Sasha! If we're lucky, you would find us a soldier built to ride up in here," my inner horny diva

spoke. Babygirl was ecstatic with the environment at the club. She was in vagina heaven.

I simply shook my head and acted as if I didn't have a second voice playing out in my mind – as if my vagina did not talk to me. I didn't want people to think I was a psycho in public. Once I paid my 20-dollar door charge and entered the club, a tall and ripped white guy approached me with a tray of drinks. His skin was tanned to perfection. His topless body was pristine with baby-oil covered muscles that flexed in my face as he spoke.

He winked and said, "Welcome to Pleasure Castle where your wish is my command. Would you like a cocktail? The house drink is free all night."

Knowing that everything free ain't good for you, I wondered what exactly was in the house drink mixture, but Babygirl could care less about the ingredients of the drink, she was more concerned with the man carrying them.

"Yeah big boy! I'll take the cock and if you ask me nicely you can have the tail any way you like it," she blurted out, sounding all irresistibly sexy. I thought I was the only one that had heard her, but from the look on the host's face, she had taken over my voice and spoke aloud.

"I think I can manage that for you," the host said as he took my hand and spun me around inspecting every inch of my skin tight outfit. "I love cat woman. Cat guuuurl! I know a good thing when I see it," he said, purring as he gawked over my appearance.

"Let's fuck him!" Babygirl begged me. This time she spoke directly to me, knowing that her satisfaction had to come with my approval.

"No way!" I quickly took the drink he offered me and almost tripped over someone trying to flee the Pleasure Castle worker. He had to have thought I was crazy for first coming on to him and then running off like some kind of scared little girl, but that was the nature of having two personalities. Oftentimes, people were left trying to figure me out. If I didn't find another delicious treat built to ride, I would definitely holler at him later, but I wasn't just going to give it up to the first man that offered me a drink, and a free drink at that. I pushed through the first crowd where men and a few lesbians were posted up gawking over the women strippers.

When I made it to the second stage, I was elated to see that I had made it just in time for King Zulu. He was only the most well-endowed stripper in the entire south. Urban Legend had it that he was fifteen inches long. According to the pictures on his website he was definitely a meat packer, no fillers or enhancers. Well, it might not have actually been fifteen inches long, but it sure looked like it could do some damage. Second to the size of his manhood, he was ripped in all the right places and had a bald head, just like I liked my men to have. He was just fine.

I managed to get a center stage seat in the crowded room. Quickly, I rummaged through my purse to find the thirty singles that I had gotten from the gas station. I made sure that I had enough singles to put those strippers to work, especially King Zulu. I was about to tip his Mandingo swinging tail at least half of the money, if not all of it off the top! As soon as I found the money, I started waving it back and forth like I was losing my mind. Within minutes, he worked his way over to me.

"Lawd. Here he comes. Don't blow it," Babygirl sang like she was about to eat her last meal. Moistening and pulsating with every movement of his body, she was like a bitch in heat.

King Zula continued his routine, sensually gyrating his pelvis, hypnotizing the women with his routine as the music blasted from the DJ booth. *Touch it- bring it - pay it - watch it - turn it - leave it - stop - format it.*

Busta Rhymes' *Touch It* beat could not keep up with the King's massive manhood swinging across the stage, visually satisfying one woman after the next. When he finally reached me, I took half of the money in my hand and just threw it at him. Then, I took a few singles that I had in my bra and thrust them into his Wonder thong.

Screaming and panting like he was a superstar, I massaged the full length of his mouth-watering groin as he performed a strip tease for me. Before I knew anything, he had me by the hand and up on the stage. Any attempt that I gave at resistance was futile in comparison to his strength. He had ten times the strength in his powerful arms than I had in my entire body.

"Come on up here, babe. Don't get scared now," he said, speaking in the microphone set that was around his ear.

"Are you crazy?" Babygirl protested when I asked to be placed back in my seat.

The crowd went wild watching him grind all over me while talking shit about it. With my legs wrapped around his waist, he said, "Let's give them a show they will not forget."

I managed to push through my lips, "Please take me back to my seat." I said the words with my mouth, but my body betrayed me as my arms wrapped tighter around his neck. My legs flung around his torso and I happily indulged in the feel of his skin against mine. I closed my eyes and allowed myself to be engulfed in his smell, touch, and feel.

"Can we have our own private show later?" Sensing my anxiety, Babygirl took over the conversation with King Zulu,

successfully pushing my own voice of reason to the back of my subconscious, once again.

"Anything for you," he answered, nibbling my ear for good measure.

She had spoken for me, so there was nothing I could do but go with the flow for the moment, at least until he put me back in my chair. Onstage, he moved in a slow, steady grind sending every inch of my flesh into a frenzy. To say that my body was on fire would be an understatement. He turned me upside down in a sixty-nine move and mimicked pleasing me orally through the fabric of my pants.

If what he did to me on the stage was a preview of what he had to offer in the bedroom, damn! His final act was to lay me down on the floor of the stage and stroke his manhood against my face. To say that I was embarrassed and aroused at the same time would be another understatement.

Before letting me go back to my seat, he placed a fat hickey on my neck and asked me to meet him backstage. He collected the remaining dollar bills from the stage floor and exited the stage with a quick bow.

The truth is, I knew better than to listen to Babygirl by coming here in the first place. I knew even better not to listen to her about going backstage, but like a love-sick puppy I was standing in front of King Zulu's dressing room within fifteen minutes after he left the stage. I had gone into the bathroom to freshen up and was ready for whatever.

Babygirl Strikes Back
Part II

by
Shani Greene-Dowdell

I couldn't believe it had been three-hundred-sixty-five days since Damon walked out on me. I hated to think about him or our relationship because it reminded me so much of my emptiness. Thinking about him took me back to the day that he broke my heart in two.

At the time, Damon had been my live in beau for two years. He meant the world to me and no one could have told me that one day I, Sasha Jordan, was not going to be his wife. I would not have believed them. I would have called them a liar and told them the truth wasn't in them. Then, I would have cursed them out on sheer principal of tainting our perfect relationship with such gossip.

The only wedge that we had between us was his pesky baby mamma and her drama. Even with Sanquetta's mess, I was confident the love that Damon and I shared for one another would overcome any mess she pitched our way. Boy, was I ever wrong!

The decision for Damon to pursue a life with his daughter and her mother came only minutes after he professed his undying love for me. First, he made love to my body and mind leaving me floating in the clouds. I could have lived on those beautiful white clouds for weeks, but I came crashing down when he rushed out of my bedroom door, never to return again. My world had not been the same since.

As much as I hated it, the man still had a permanent residence in my heart and so far, I had been unsuccessful in evicting him from that space.

Against my better judgment, as I stood in front of King Zulu's dressing room door and raised my hand to knock, I allowed my mind to travel back to the day that often played out like a vivid movie, over and over again, down to the last scene. The day Damon left.

On this particular day, I walked through my foyer after a long day at work to find Damon sitting on the sofa watching an X-rated movie. He usually worked third shift, so I was surprised to find him awake, much less sitting in the living room watching porn.

I rolled my eyes in displeasure of him watching the video in the middle of the day, without me, and walked in the opposite direction of him. I knew those movies turned him on something silly and soon he would be ready to relieve some of that frustration with me. Quite frankly, I wasn't in the mood. After a drama-filled day at the bank office, all I wanted to do was blend up a strawberry daiquiri, lay down, and read a good book.

"Hey babe!" Damon jumped at the sound of the door closing behind me. He pressed the stop button on the DVD player and stood. "How was your day, Sasha?"

I looked over my shoulder to see that he was practically on my heels. "Like every other day in that hellhole, Damon! What should make today any different? Those bitches, I tell you, I'm going to hurt somebody one day."

I placed my keys on the key holder and proceeded to walk into the kitchen. I worked as a financial advisor for Gold Financial and in between irritating customers and my gossipy coworkers it took all that I had in me to remain professional.

I continued, "Kenzie did everything within her power to dodge doing some real work today, leaving everything on me as usual. That woman knows how to get on my last nerve. Oh, and just wait until I tell you what the heifer had the nerve to tell me today."

Stroking a few loose strands of my hair back into place, Damon listened attentively as I prepared to spit out everything on my mind. I released my tensions from my heart and spirit onto him daily, and he allowed it. He was very good about listening to me go on tangents about my problems on the job. That was Damon, always lending a good ear. He seemed genuinely concerned, as if he wished he could take my pain away.

Kenzie, on the other hand, was my lazy coworker who always kept some office chaos brewing. She did as little work as possible because she was too busy spreading rumors. However, she always managed to put herself in a good light for higher management and never missed the monthly performance bonus that I pulled the weight for. Today, her clown performance included getting into my personal business and I was not having it. I overheard her telling Linda that Damon had been seeing Sanquetta behind my back. She said that she 'had spotted them out around town having dinner without the baby, so Damon must be cheating on me.' She had said that to anyone that would listen in the office with no regard as to whether or not it would get back to me.

That lying heifer didn't know what my man was doing! Just last week, she told me that Linda's husband was cheating on her with their neighbor, so what gives? And my question to her was, 'How do you always know whose husband is fucking who?' After I asked her that, I watched her simmer over the question, but she never responded.

Tired to the bone, I plopped my briefcase down onto the kitchen table, washed my hands in the sink, plugged in the blender, and pulled some strawberries out of the refrigerator. When Damon reached up and pulled the Absolute down from the cabinet, I could see his sexy abs glistening. They glistened as if he had just showered and rubbed lotion on his body. I was in a salty mood, but not too salty to notice my man.

He was the only man that I'd had the privilege of dating that took the time to lotion, and on special occasions, oil his entire body from head to toe every time he took a shower. I loved that about him. To top it off, his confident swagger, bare muscular chest, and the unmistakable hypnotizing bulge from his boxers was extra noticeable at that moment.

As I stood over the sink preparing my relaxing potion, I felt his hands gently massage my shoulders. His hard body pressed snuggly against my rear. The command he had over me relieved more tension than any session I could have had with my massage therapist. I gently laid my head back so that it was resting comfortably on his chest. Even though I didn't necessarily feel like being intimate at the moment, I closed my eyes, took a deep breath, and enjoyed the massage my man was graciously giving me.

After what seemed like the best massage that I'd ever received and a few smooth daiquiris, I was feeling good. Kenzie and her mess were the furthest things from my mind. Damon and I had made our way into the living room and he'd turned back on the video that he was watching when I came in. I laid across his lap awake but with my eyes closed resting.

He muted the TV and asked, "Are you going to tell me what was bothering you so much from work? What did Kenzie say to you?"

I sat up on the couch looking him square in the eyes. Before I could open my mouth to give him the details of my day, Babygirl took over the conversation. *"We...we can talk about it later. Right now, I want you to make love to me."*

Before I parted my lips to say another word, he raised my skirt exposing my pink thongs while he softly nibbled on my ear. "Oh, you want me to make *love* to you, huh? Well, I can definitely do that. In fact, that is all I have wanted to do all day." He stood and gently eased my pink thongs down my legs and returned to my neck for a kiss. His lips felt heavenly against my skin. Gingerly, he moved his powerful hands to my plump breasts, caressing them passionately.

I somehow managed to swallow the lump in my throat and said, "I want you so bad."

My issues with Kenzie could wait. There was no way I was going to discuss her anyway with Damon watching porn, aroused, and ready to make love to me. If I could help it, I would be the only woman on his mind when he was sexually aroused.

Allowing his hands to roam all over my body, they ended at my juice pot. My swollen lips welcomed his soft and warm fingers and rode each wave of pleasure as they danced across my swollen bulb. He rubbed me into a frenzy applying just the right amount of pressure to send me into finger-vagina utopia. I surrendered to this soothing assault and leaned back onto the couch. He was in total control. His gigantic hands were one of the attractions that drew me to him. I love a man with big hands.

"Mmmmmm," I let out a loud moan as he stroked Babygirl's bud the way she loved him to do. My body trembled, as she released a river of her special love juice. Round one was officially over. I loved that my man could bring me to climax without actually using his God-given sexual tools.

He licked his fingers and smacked the juices off of them. "You taste so good, Sasha," he said, and I could feel my body tremble to the decibels of his baritone voice.

"I want to feel you inside of me, now!" I demanded, writhing on the couch up against him ready to reach the highest of sexual highs once again. It was amazing how fast the tables had turned on me. When I walked in the door, I didn't even want to be bothered with him. Twenty minutes later, and I was practically begging him to penetrate me. That was the kind of power that he had over Babygirl, a name that he gave to her during a lovemaking session. I was strong enough to resist, but Babygirl was weak.

"Slow your roll," he said with a bode of confidence. "I see I wasn't the only one with a lot of pent up sexual frustration today." He smiled, knowing he had me exactly where he wanted me. Desperate. I loved the vulnerability, as well. Was there anything about him that I didn't love, though?

"Whatever," I told him, making an attempt to sound blasé. Inside, I knew he was about to rock my world just like he did every time we made love.

He stood me up onto my wobbly legs and swooped me into his arms. A flash of his charismatic grin confirmed that he was the only man that could make me cum without even touching me.

The journey to my bedroom was a long one. We left our clothes on the kitchen floor. When he laid me down on the kitchen table to eat his dinner, naturally, I was the only thing on the menu. That man pinned me against the table and sucked my neck hungrily. He kissed my lips with the same fever as he had the first time we made love, caressing my tongue with his.

The deep moans that escaped from his throat made my heart melt. The simple thought that he was incensed with passion for me drove me wild. My lower region was about to explode with when he licked a trail from my chin down to my swollen bulb. My eyes fixated on his baldhead as he moved his tongue back and forth assaulting Babygirl until I mentally felt as if I would pass out from pleasure.

"Oh, my damn! Damon, baby! Damon! I'm about to cum," I screamed as orgasmic waves washed over my petite brown frame.

Three hours later, I had napped and was lying in bed entangled in the covers next to Damon watching him sleep. I could not get enough of my Chocolate King. He was all that a woman could ask for, need, or desire in and out of the sheets. It was days like those that reminded me why I surrendered my heart to him in the first place. At that very moment, I counted my blessings that I was able to come home to him each and every day.

I nestled up close to him until I felt safe in his muscular embrace. His massive body completely covered mine and I fit perfectly into his grooves as if we were made for each other. I would have spent the rest of my life just like that, if I could have.

He stirred from his slumber. His first motion was to wrap his arms around my waist and pull me as close as we could possibly get without meshing into one. It was not long before I could feel his body hardening against mine. I took this as an opportunity to position myself atop of him. Straddling him, I was ready to fulfill his each and every desire. Our bed of heated passion was momentarily cooled when the house phone rang.

It was sitting on the night stand, so I vividly could see that the caller ID displayed Sanquetta Newman's number. It was Daman's baby mama. She was calling from her cell phone.

"It's Sanquetta," I told him, feeling as if I had suddenly lost all interest in being on top of him.

Sanquetta had a way of making me burn with envy. She was the one that had his child. She was the only person that could call and ruin a perfectly good evening for us. Sometimes she would do just that, simply because she wanted to.

"Let the answering machine get it. I'll call her back tomorrow," he said, pulling me back on top of him. "Come on, babe. I want you right back where you belong."

After the answering machine message and a beep, Sanquetta's irritating voice sang out, "Damon, this is San. It is urgent that I talk to you. Call me as soon as you get this message!"

"Everything is urgent to Sanquetta," I said, as Damon pulled me down onto his shaft. He entered me extremely hard as if his entrance would erase all memory of Sanquetta's call that interrupted our passionate evening.

"Yeah, and me making love to you again tonight is just as urgent." His thrusts were paced and calculated. I joined his rhythm and could soon feel my core coming to a meltdown.

I was just about to release when the phone rang again. This time, without hesitation, I pressed the "Busy Tone" button on the phone, which quieted the rings.

Still stroking the depth of my core and causing me to gasp with every stroke, he said, "I talked to Cherise right before you got home from work this evening and everything was fine. I'll call her back in a little while."

I attempted to enjoy my man again, but the phone rang for the third and fourth times in four minutes. On the fourth call, before the first ring could even complete, I yanked the phone up from the receiver. It was true that Sanquetta was a bugaboo, but she had never called back to back like that.

"Hello?" I answered the call with a chilling attitude. Damon was still inside of me stroking me slowly, running his finger up and down my back, pleading with his eyes for me to hurry up and get rid of whoever was on the phone.

"Hello Sasha. Put Damon on the phone," she was blunt and spoke in a polite but demanding tone.

Becoming tense, I let out a long sigh of disgust. "Damon is sleeping. What do you need?" Note, I asked her what she needed because as far as I was concerned she wasn't getting what she wanted, my man. All of my movements stopped, but Damon was making love to me as if I did not have a phone attached to my hand speaking to his child's mother.

"Look Sasha. Put him on the phone. It is important," she said sounding a little more humbled than I'd ever heard her sound. "Cherise..." she stopped midsentence and sighed, as if to tell me the problem would go against all of her Baby Mama Principles.

I was two seconds away from hanging up on her so that I could ride the orgasmic waves building within me properly, but I wanted to make sure nothing was wrong with my stepdaughter to be.

"Is Cherise okay?" I asked. Mind you, Damon was sensually stroking my core something sensuously. I didn't know how much more I could take before I blew my cover on the phone and Sanquetta would know that we were making love while I was talking to her.

Sanquetta must have known that I was not going to give Damon the phone unless she had a valid reason for calling so late in the evening, so she spit it out.

Her voice cracked as she said, "No, Sasha, she is not all right. She has been admitted to the hospital and has been asking for her daddy for over an hour! Damon needs to come to Shady Memorial Hospital right away."

I could tell by her cracking voice and desperation that she was being truthful. She had never lied about Cherise's health. I rolled over onto the bed breaking the intimate contact between Damon and I.

I said, "Oh, my God! What is the matter? Is it her asthma?" I fired off a barrage of questions trying to find out Cherise's status. By that time Damon was sitting up square in the bed with a puzzled look on his face.

"Yes, it is her asthma and it is really bad this time. So would you please just let me speak to Damon?"

I quickly handed Damon the phone without further interrogation. Needless to stay, after a quick update, he hung up the phone, got dressed, and left for the hospital.

"Should I ride with you?" I asked as I threw on some sweat pants and a tee shirt. "I will drive."

"No, I'll give you a call once I get there," he said anxiously, kissing my cheek as he headed out of the front door.

I guessed he didn't want to take me along for fear that Sanquetta and I would end up fighting over Cherise's hospital bed. I would never do anything like that, and I told him as much, but I didn't argue with him. It was much more important that he got there as fast as he could so that Cherise would know that her father was there for her. I kissed him goodbye. He never stepped foot back into our home that we shared after that night.

When he finally answered his cell phone a week later, he explained that seeing his daughter in the hospital, with all of the tubes hooked up to her, made him realize how fast he could lose her. He wanted to be able to spend more time with his daughter and be a bigger part of her life. He explained that he loved me and would never forget me, but that if he had to be with Sanquetta in order to be there one-hundred percent for his daughter that leaving me was a sacrifice that he was willing to make. I had been sacrificed. He wanted to be able to be with his daughter everyday and watch her grow up. Kiss her knee when she scraped it and help her with her homework. He wanted to be there for her when she was sick. He didn't like the fact that he had to be tracked down to be told that his daughter had stopped breathing. He wanted to be by her side to give her his last breath, if need be.

I tried to reason, and even begged. I told him that he could be all of those things for Cherise with me as his wife. However, his mind was made up. His resolve was solid. When I hung up the phone, I was officially single. I fell onto my bed and poured my heart into my pillow.

What started out as a nice trip down memory lane was interrupted by harsh reality. I had come to grips that sitting around the house moping could not mend my broken heart. I was forced to enter into a new chapter of my life. Tonight, a flaming sexscapade with the sexy King Zulu would be chapter one. Backstage standing in front of King Zulu's door, I put on a smile and knocked.

Babygirl Strikes Back
Part III

by
Shani Greene-Dowdell

Standing at King Zulu's door reminiscing about Damon had given me some sort of finality about that relationship. It was definitely over, and I was definitely about to get my world rocked by a stripper.

When he opened his door, I looked up to see the tallest, darkest, finest chocolate chip I had ever seen in my life. Yes, his physique would even put Damon's to shame. To look into his eyes was to be hypnotized by an aura so familiar I felt like I was having yet another trip down memory lane with one of the best lovers I never had. I felt like I had slept walked to his dressing room and was still dreaming. His stage presence did not do justice to the real man up close and personal.

Instead of a formal greeting, he picked me up off my feet and kissed me long and deep on the lips. The gesture caught me off guard, because the kiss was like one a man would plant on a long lost lover after a long separation, not someone that he was going to bang out for one night and then forget her name. I pushed that thought to the back of my head and just reveled in the moment. It was what it was, a one night stand, so I would not allow myself to make any more or any less of it.

He carried me over to his plush sofa and sat me down gently like a piece of fine china fresh out of the box and then returned to the door to lock it. I began to explain that it was not everyday that I ran backstage with a stripper for a quickie. As well, I wanted to know that it was not everyday that he brought a different woman back stage.

"I...um...I..."

Before I could speak, he placed a finger over my lips as if he predicted my ambivalence.

"First time for everything," he said in a throaty voice, taking three steps back from the couch and methodically performing another strip tease for me. He removed his black and gray Wonder thong, the only piece of clothing covering his body after his performance. When the thong hit the floor, I knew I was in trouble. Good trouble, but serious trouble nonetheless.

I started to think of ways to get out of the bind I found myself in, because it was obvious I'd bitten off more than I could ever chew, even on a good day. "Um...I think I better...um get going. This was....um not such a good idea. I don't really know you and um..." I snuggled my purse up closer under my arm and held up a finger as I started thinking of ways to make it to the door with my pride intact.

To hell if I was about to let him stick even half of his tool up into my tight body. I wasn't trying to be up in the ER tonight with a repositioned uterus, nor was I trying to get ripped open like that the first time after not having sex for a year.

Sensing my ambivalence, he took my purse from me and sat it down on the coffee table and said, "Don't let the size worry you. I know how to use it, and I promise to be gentle with you." He took me by the hand and maneuvered my tiny hand onto his enormous rod. "Go ahead and touch him. Blue won't hurt you."

"Blue? Is that what you call him?" I laughed, feeling a little more comfortable because we had something in common. We both had nicknames for our sexual organs. As I made myself comfortable rubbing him, he allowed his hands to wander over my breasts.

Removing his hands from my breasts, he stroked his hard flesh along with me. "Yes, that's what I call him."

"Why do you call him that? I would think his name would be The Big Dipper or something like that." We both chuckled at my attempt at humor.

"Well because most of the time I end up with blue balls after women get me all roused up and then run for cover once they see what I'm working with.

"Well hell. We ain't running!" Babygirl imposed herself again to let me know with the quickness that we were going for the gusto. She was anxious to have him inside of her and was not keeping that fact a secret. "Woman up Sasha! We can end this one year drought tonight with a biggest and possibly the best dick we have ever had. What are you waiting on?" She fussed and I was glad he could not hear her rambling on.

I couldn't deny that I was months past ready to end my no-sex streak. This man was about as sexy as they came, so I figured he would be just what I needed to get over Damon. I began to sensually stroke Blue, moving my hand from the tip down the shaft to the root. Once I had turned up the heat by placing a kiss on the tip, King Zulu trembled under my touch, obviously enjoying the pleasure from my hand and lips.

He pulled me to my feet and kissed me hard on the lips. When the kiss broke, I said confidently, "Well Mr. Blue, get ready to meet Babygirl."

I removed the straps from my cat suit and wiggled out of it, anxious to feel my naked flesh against his. At that moment,

I was glad Babygirl chose this outfit because I hardly ever wore underwear with it.

My perfectly shaven kitten must have purred for attention, because he immediately dropped to his knees and kissed my navel. He worked his way to my thighs taking the time to place tender kisses in meticulous circles as he descended. Gently, he manipulated Babygirl's bulb into his mouth rhythmically moving his tongue over her and then sucking her ever so lightly. With every stroke of his tongue another wave of orgasmic pleasure came over me until his face was covered with juice. His tongue soon became more than I could handle. My legs buckled and I fell back onto the softness of couch.

Reveling in the fact that he'd literally knocked me off of my feet, his face turned up into a satisfied, devilish grin. Laying on top of me, he placed one of my legs at a time over his shoulder. He planted another of his signature kisses on my lips.

Admiring the fine specimen that mounted me, I was almost too far gone to remember the fact that he was packing a sizable package. When the reminder rubbed up against my pussy as he grinded his pelvis into mine, I tried to squirm my way out of the compromising position. He must have read my apprehension, because he said, "You will enjoy every inch of Blue. I'll be gentle with you, baby. I promise."

He stood up and walked over to his closet where he opened his duffle bag and retrieved a box of Magnum XXXL. Once he'd applied a condom, rubbed a generous amount of lube on it, and walked back over to me I wanted this man in the worst way. He placed the remaining condoms on the coffee table.

Thank God for lube, I thought as he applied it. I was sure that I was going to burn in hell for thanking God for lubricant to use on a one-night stand, but I needed all the blessings that my tight pussy could get. After all, God must have shown favor to King Zulu because he was blessed with endowment.

He reclaimed his place on top of me and kissed me gently, again like an old lover. Being there with him at that moment felt right. Slowly and meticulously, he eased himself inside of me inch by inch, stroking first with the tip and then easing in with more and more of his shaft with each pump. He traveled deeper and deeper into my abyss until he could not go any further. When my body had stretched to the max, he found a rhythm that was made for the two of us.

In attempt to take all that he had to offer like a real woman, I bit down on my lip until the mixture of pleasure and pain was too much for me to hold inside.

"Oh...Zulu...Fuck!" I cried out. Yes, I was crying real tears as he heartily tore through my body with his sensually rhythmic strokes.

He smothered my screams with a kiss that could mask any pain. "Damn, you feel so good, girl," he whispered right before moving his kisses to my neck.

Once I was comfortable with the eleven or so inches I was receiving, I attempted to match his thrusts with the same fervor. However, between his length and muscular body on top of me, I was pinned into place. All I could do was gently slide my tongue down his throat as he kissed and made love to me. Even though it felt like what we were sharing was more than just a fluke one-night stand, I was simply happy to receive all that he had to offer me for a night.

"You feel so good Sasha, too good," he said before running his tongue over the wanting skin of my neck, once again. He was a kisser that loved to use his tongue.

"You feel, damn..." I paused midsentence because I didn't remember telling him my name. Before I could mention the coincidence of him saying my name, he stood up taking me with him. Never once did he allow his throbbing pole to leave my sugary core. He then turned around and sat down on the sofa with me in position to ride him.

"Take your time, baby. I got you," he whispered as I eased down onto his full length. It hurt at first, but with his coaching and gentle maneuvering I settled into a nice and slow pace atop of him.

It was not long before, again, pleasure overtook the pain and light moans constantly escaped my throat. I came continuously like a leaky faucet when he massaged my clit as I stroked him, heightening the pleasure of fucking him. His pace quickened, so I knew he was about to cum, as well. That was when I straddled him with my arms wrapped around his neck. I thrust my body hard down onto his, anxious to pleasure him as he had so selflessly done for me.

"Oh right there, Sasha. Keep it right there! Damn you feel so good girl. You feel good," he said between deep moans, jamming his manhood into my honey pot faster and harder.

I put every muscle in my back to work to give him the best orgasm ever. If I never saw him again after tonight, he would remember the way I rode him for a long time. Within seconds, we climaxed together and collapsed onto the couch. Five minutes later, I lay limp on his chest in the same position I was in after his orgasm. After our breaths finally returned to normal I sat up and looked him square in the eyes and asked, "How do you know my name?"

His mood turned completely serious and he said, "So you really don't remember me?" The puzzled look on my face told him I didn't, so he continued, "tenth grade. Mr. Calhoun's class."

"Huh?"

"I used to carry your books from Mr. Calhoun's class to Mrs. Threadmill's class. Remember me now?"

It was at that moment that his big black eyes and thick eyebrows jarred my memory, but he couldn't be...him.

"Please, say it ain't so. Marlon Jackson?" I asked ambivalently as I pushed away from him.

He simply smiled and pulled me back into his arms. "The one and only."

My eyes brightened like a kid in a candy store. I actually felt like I was back in tenth grade again with a crush on him, but too shy to say so. When he would offer to carry my books, I would just let him. But I didn't let him know that I liked him too.

"Oh my God, I had the biggest crush on you," I admitted.

In one swift move, he flipped me over onto my back so that I was horizontal on the couch and climbed on top of me kissing tiny circles around my face and neck.

"Not as big as the one I had on you."

"I can't believe we just..." I looked away at the wall, ashamed that I'd just had sex with a man that I didn't know I knew. I silently cursed Babygirl because she had a way of getting me into the worst situations.

"Yes, I just made love to you Sasha. I knew exactly what I wanted to do to you when I spotted you in the crowd. Please tell me that you don't have any regrets now." He tugged my chin so that our eyes met again, and I gave him my undivided attention.

"No regrets, Marlon," I said cutting through any barrier that I had put up. "My have you grown into one hell of a man.

I mean you really have *grown* into a fine specimen," I teased, for good measure, letting him know that I really had no regrets that the stripper that I'd just had one hour of passionate sex with was him.

He laughed and said, "I'm the same as I was in high school. Haven't grown an inch. The only thing that has changed is a few muscles, my clothes, and my status."

Remembering how attracted we were to each other in high school but didn't tell each other then, I said, "Marlon, I want you to know this is the first time I have done something like this, but I have been attracted to King Zulu since the first time I saw you perform in Birmingham. I didn't know you were *my* Marlon from DJ High School."

"You don't have to explain anything to me. I did what I've been wanting to do since I first laid eyes on you years ago. You have not changed one bit, by the way. Just so you know, to see your pretty face, I've been banking at Gold Financial for the past year."

"Mr. M. E. Jackson," I said as realization came over me. "I've always wondered why he, well you, stood in my line even if there were other lines open with no customers. Wow! And that was you the whole time, King Zulu, Marlon Jackson...you look so different out of your three-piece suits."

With a nervous laugh, he said, "Yeah, my stripper attire is a little different, huh? Would you say that is a good or bad thing?"

"It's great!"

"So what would you say about us spending some more time together, but the next time maybe an official date at your favorite restaurant?"

I knew that my cheeks had to have turned flush red when he asked me out. I reached up and touched my hair and said, "Sure. I can't believe what just happened – me and you?"

I could not think of anything better to say, because it had all happened so fast that I really could not believe I had just had sex with my tenth grade crush. Coming down off of my sexual high, the first seed of love was planted in my heart at that very moment. His revelations about having "made love" to me like he wanted to do years ago had me burning up with desire, even more than I had when I first came backstage to meet him.

"Believe it baby, because now that I've felt your body flesh to flesh it will be hard to get rid of me." He gave me another devilish grin, picked up another condom from his coffee table, slipped it on, and thrust his dick inside of me.

We made love until sunrise and he put it on me so good that it was at least two weeks before I could walk a straight line. As far as Babygirl was concerned, Blue would never get another case of blue balls again. She would make sure of it.

King Zulu still performs at Pleasure Castle Thursday night through Saturday night, but now Babygirl and I have front row seats and a permanent backstage pass, just a few perks of becoming Mrs. Jackson. But really, what were the odds that Babygirl would talk me into a night of fulfilling her lustful desires and I would find the real love of my life in the process?

That's right, Mr. Jackson made an honest woman out of me. I can be sexual and free with no regrets because *I'ze married now!*

Shani Greene-Dowdell's concept for creating the Mocha Chocolate series was simple: to bring the hottest fantasies alive for responsible and passionate creatures, both men and women alike, to enjoy. *Babygirl Blue* takes internal passion to another level exploring how sexual energy can take on a life of its own and guide both women and men around on a leash. It was a fun and sexy story of a woman dealing with her alter personality - vagina.

She is also the author of *Keepin' It Tight* and Secrets of a Kept Woman, and created Nayberry Publications to publish her books and other authors. Visit her online at www.shanibooks.com or www.nayberrypublications.com.

Roommates by Niyah Moore

Cidnee

Micah unbuttoned his black long-sleeved button up shirt as soon as I closed the front door to our apartment. It was completely dark, so I turned the light above our heads on. He took off the shirt, leaving on the white tank top he had underneath. He proceeded to take off his shoes in silence, and then left the articles recklessly at the door, a pet peeve I dreaded. It didn't matter how many times I told him to at least line the shoes up against the wall neatly, he didn't.

I always took off my shoes at the door too, but I took them to my bedroom closet. Nothing was worse than coming home in the middle of the night and losing my balance over Timberland Boots and dress shirts. I tried not to be his maid, but I did a lot of cleaning up after him, fussing all the while. Tonight, I wasn't in the mood for any of that.

Lingering through the house was a hint of the jasmine incense I'd burned before we left. I went into the kitchen to make myself an apple martini; something I did every time we came back from hanging out late with our mutual friends. It helped me to sleep better somehow.

He entered the kitchen behind me and watched. I poured and then shook up the mixture with ice. I figured he had enough to drink at the bar earlier, but I asked anyway, "Do you want some?"

"I don't need any more to drink."

I couldn't help but notice how his eyes glanced at me, a look I've never seen nestled in those light brown eyes of his. They traveled down to my legs and stayed there. I was a thick girl, between sizes, a twelve at the moment. I wasn't exactly plus size and I definitely wasn't thin. I was curvy, but a few cupcakes away from being too heavy. All my life, I had been given the sister or best friend title. I was just "cool" to every male I came across.

Even when Micah noticed that I was aware of his odd stare, he didn't look away. His eyes locked with mine, as if he didn't mind me catching him. I could feel my golden brown skin actually turning crimson. I poured the cold drink into a martini glass, hoping he didn't catch my embarrassment. I looked back at him to see what exactly he was staring at.

I had to admit, I wasn't oblivious to the fact that Micah was fine. I simply chose to ignore him. He was tall with smooth ebony dark skin. He was an excellent dresser and also a serious hoe-magnet. I mean, seriously, every woman he dated did whatever he wanted them to do. And every single one of them looked like fashion models. To see him gawking at me, as if I was a nice tall glass of ice water in the middle of the Mohave Desert, perplexed me.

Micah's muscular chiseled body and handsome strong features were hard enough to ignore day after day, and at times, I felt like I was melting. After living with him for so long, I never thought he would be staring at me with such fascination.

Maybe he wasn't digging me. Maybe I was making it all up in my head. "What?" I asked when he wouldn't take his eyes off me.

"You look nice tonight in that short black dress."

I laughed at the way he leaned up against the door frame of the kitchen. He looked as if he was really feeling the liquor. "You must be drunk, Roomy."

"I am smashed," he owned up slowly, "but..." He pointed his index finger in the air as if he had an idea, but forgot it that quickly.

I laughed at him again and sipped my drink. "I think you're beyond that."

"You might be right," he said resting against the black granite counter. "On the other hand, I am sober enough to think clearly."

For two years, after college, we had been straight real roomies, our rooms on opposite ends of the apartment. We never flirted with one another, or danced around the sex subject ever. Certain topics were almost forbidden and definitely unspoken. We shared friends and went out with them every weekend.

I changed the subject by asking, "What are you wearing to work tomorrow?"

"Don't know," he shrugged.

"If you could wear jerseys and jeans to work, you would."

"True. Don't forget about the baseball cap."

"Yo, most def, and it has to be so low where no one can see your eyes."

"I have a confession," he said out of no where.

"What's that?"

He didn't answer with words; instead he came to me, took me by my waist, and planted a soft kiss on my lips. It was quick, no tongue, and it was the softest kiss I ever had.

I looked at him as if he had lost his mind. I pushed him away with my left hand. "That was nice, but why did you do that?"

He smiled handsomely. "I just want to touch you all over. Is your body as soft as it looks?"

This tingly sensation made the tiny hairs on the back of my neck stand straight up. Confusion immediately set in. He had to be playing some mean joke.

"What?" I asked to make sure he just said what I thought he uttered.

"Are you attracted to me, Cidnee?"

"Are you attracted to me?" I asked right back quickly.

"I asked you first..."

I drank the rest of the drink and placed the glass on the black granite countertop.

He trapped my body between his and the counter with his long arms. "So, are you attracted to me?"

I searched his eyes with a frown still on my face. "No."

"No?" he asked raising his eyebrows.

He was making me nervous as hell. His confident arrogance was enticing me for some reason. He knew his power and he was playing on it.

"Are you attracted to me?" I asked again.

"It's like...the sexual desire I have for you is strong, There are days when I want to fuck you hard, right here on this countertop." He bit on his lower lip as he rested is nose against mine.

I swallowed the hard lump in my throat. Maybe he wasn't playing with me. "A-a-r-r-r-e you serious?" I stuttered.

"They're just dreams I have," he said moving his right hand to my hair.

He moved his hand through my scalp. My eyes didn't blink one bit. The desire was clear as he licked those lips again and stared at me with a gleam of curiosity. "I want my dream to become a reality. Can you help me with that?"

I removed his hand from my hair. "You're crazy. Quit gassing me."

"I'm not gassing you...Maybe we can make that dream come to life tonight, right now."

"Micah, you can't be serious."

"Cidnee..."

I got out of his reach and made another apple martini. I felt my insides shaking. He was turning me on, but my heart was racing so fast I thought I was going to have a heart attack.

He touched my back rubbing lightly and that sensation up my spine intensified.

"If you need to talk to me about your breakup, you can. You don't have to sleep with me to redeem yourself," I said. He had just broken up with his girlfriend a little over a few weeks previously. I didn't want to be used for some type of ill rebound or to get her off of his mind.

He watched how my lips wrapped around that glass. My tongue licked the sugar off the rim.

Without acknowledging my statement, he said, "Okay, so back to my dream becoming a reality..."

"You're crazy," I repeated waving my hand in the air.

His dimples deepened as his smile widened. "If you only knew..."

I laughed nervously. "I'm your roommate."

"Is there some rule that states roommates can't enjoy one another?"

"There are roommate frontlines that you just don't cross."

"I don't think a man can live with a woman and not be attracted to her, unless he just wasn't attracted to her at all."

"And you're not attracted to me, at all, so quit playing."

"You think I'm playing."

He licked his lips slowly and leaned in to kiss me again.

"I don't want you to do this," I said pulling away from him.

"Why?"

"I don't want a quickie."

He laughed as if I said the funniest thing in the world. "Hmmm, let's see. I don't know what a quickie is. I do take my time, and I promise you'll be screaming my name."

I quivered under his touch as if I was having a pre-orgasm. "You think I'll be screaming?" I asked mesmerized.

"Oh yes, you'll be screaming my name."

I narrowed my eyes and poked him in his chest. "You're so damned cocky."

He lifted my body up off the tiled floor and placed me on the counter as if I weighed very little. My eyes lit up with excitement as he took the glass out of my hands. He kissed me hard while placing his hands up my dress. He took my bottom in his big hands and grabbed it firmly. A smile eased across his face as he felt around my black thong.

"I had a Brazilian wax earlier," I said reading his mind.

"Feels good," he said gently moving his fingers to my clit.

"What exactly are you trying to do to me, Micah?" I whispered against his ear.

Micah

I hadn't always been attracted to Cidnee. Some unexplainable magnetic attraction seemed as if it happened overnight, and I couldn't believe that I was finally easing inside of her juicy walls. She thrust her hips into me immediately, gushing all over me like a water sprinkler turned on full blast. I bit on my lower lip while moving in and out of her.

"Stop!" she screamed pushing me away.

I frowned because she only allowed me to give her four pumps. She reached for her drink and gulped the rest before hopping off the counter.

"What? What's the matter?" I asked holding onto my dripping dick.

She said, "Follow me."

I followed her to the living room. She sat on the couch and flipped on the TV with the remote control.

"Keep it off," I demanded feeling myself growing sick of getting the run around.

"Okay," she said and turning it back off.

She placed the remote on the coffee table. My dick was wondering why she let me in her sweet spot for such a short time and then pushed me out so quickly. I was throbbing ready to get back into her suppleness.

"Can you unzip me?" she asked observing my dazed state.

I unzipped her dress plenty of times, but never in a dark room and not after playing with the idea of having sex. The light from the moon came through the white curtains and illuminated her golden caramel-colored skin. She looked so damn sexy, yet she wasn't aware of just how sexy she truly was.

I tried to unzip it quickly, but the zipper was stuck. I found myself sweating by the time I finally got the zipper down. She revealed her thick body, which was beautiful. She had a few stretch marks, even though she hadn't had children, but it wasn't a turn off. Her imperfections were breathtakingly striking. I drank her in slowly from head to toe, but she covered herself with her arms self-consciously.

"Why are we in the dark?" I asked. "I want to see your sexy body."

She pushed me onto the couch and straddled me. "I like the dark."

I inhaled the strawberries and crème body butter she put on every inch of her skin after showering. I kissed her lips easily, slowly, and gently. We parted.

"Yo, I'm digging your apple martini kisses," I said and meant every word of it. She tasted so good.

She kissed me again. I don't know how long we kissed, but it was awhile. I adjusted a couch pillow behind my head while caressing her back. I held onto her waist as her tongue twisted in and out of my mouth.

She was uncomfortable with my hands pinching on her thick waist, so she moved them. Like the rebel I was, I moved my hands back to her waist and caressed every bit of her flesh. I loved how soft she felt.

She made her way to my neck, leaving my lips alone for the moment. My whole body was feeling tingly, almost like goose bumps. I didn't want this night to ever end.

"Is that your spot?" she asked sucking lightly.

My toes curled beyond my control. "Damn," I whispered.

She sucked a little harder and then her tongue made small circles. I moved my hands to her plump breasts, removed that bra, and stared up at her double D firm golden breasts.

"Wow..." I said.

I sat up and put my mouth on one, making my tongue search her nipple. She moaned as I took the other one as well. Then it was back to her lips. She helped me take off my tank top and pants. Before I let her touch me again, I took her hands and crossed them behind her back, while kissing the rest of the way to my bedroom.

I laid her on my bed. She moaned as I kissed her all over every scar and mole. She was insecure and tried to cover up her waistline, but I removed her hands, kissing what she was trying to conceal. It was too late to hide from me. I had already fallen in love with the way she looked naked.

She had a butterfly tattoo on her upper thigh and I licked it. "Have you ever...wondered what it would be like?" I asked.

"Wondered what would be like?" She got up on her knees and placed her hands around my neck.

"Have you ever thought about fucking me?"

She closed her eyes as if my touch made her feel so good. "No..."

"Cidnee.... Tonight, I don't want you to hold back."

I grabbed the back of her head pushing my tongue deep into her mouth. She moaned softly as I tugged her bottom lip towards me.

"Whew." She blew out air from her lips. "Are you sure this is something you want to do?"

"Positive. Touch me."

Her shaking nervous hands felt like fire every time she touched me. I moved my hands to her nipples. I must've sent a chilling sensation up her spine because she quivered as if I had just performed magic. Her hands took hold of my dick.

"Damn Micah," she said stroking the hardness that was poking up against her stomach.

"What?" I frowned, but then raised one eyebrow when I noticed she was referring to my size.

"I should've known you were this endowed. The way you have these women going crazy..." She shook her head and licked her lips, "You're huge." She moved her hands up and down along my shaft.

Her breathing picked up as my tongue rolled over her neck. She made a trail of kisses down my chest until she reached the very tip of my dick, almost teasing me. She licked me slow, like a lollipop, took me into her wet mouth, and sucked.

My back arched. I closed my eyes, and opened them quickly to make sure this wasn't a dream. I didn't want to cum yet, so I pushed her back on the bed.

Taking her feet into my hands, I kissed my way all the way up to the inside of her thick thighs. My tongue explored all around her, and even inside of her.

"Micah," she said out of breath, "I want you now."

"Right now?" I teased making my tongue go around her clit rapidly.

"Now."

"Are you sure you can handle me? You acted like you couldn't handle me in the kitchen a moment ago."

I reached into my lower dresser drawer and got a condom. She took it from me because she wanted to put it on. I moved my mouth to her breast.

"Quit playing," she said taking her breast out my mouth. "I need to feel you inside of me right now."

She pulled me down on top of her roughly as soon as she had the condom on. I fit snugly inside. She winced digging her nails into my arms as I moved in and out of her gently. She licked my collarbone like she did the sugar from her martini. She grabbed both of her legs and said, "Push me to my limit, please."

I pushed her legs until they touched my headboard. She was flexible. I thrust slowly, deeper and deeper. Each time her moan became louder.

"Shhhh," I hushed.

"Sorry, it's just that you feel so good."

She had to put a pillow over her face to stop herself from being too loud. She came so hard that she wet up my sheets straight through to my mattress.

I rubbed her arm softly. She looked angelic while I stared down at her. I placed a kiss on her forehead and then kissed her cheek while holding onto my orgasm. I couldn't cum yet. She stirred a little. I could feel my heart drumming through my chest as I moved my kiss to her lips.

"You're beautiful."

She opened her eyes and she looked shocked when I said those words, but then her right hand found its way to the side of my face. I kissed her deeply. She kissed me back matching my intensity. She was breathing just as hard as I was.

"What are you doing?" she asked when she noticed I stopped moving inside of her.

"Shhhh," I replied kissing her again.

She made her tongue flicker in and out of my mouth. I put my hand between her thighs and began rubbing. She took hold of that same hand and made me touch her deeper.

I entered her soft tight spot again, her nails digging into my back, and her mild moans turned into screams. I could hardly catch my breath as I gave her the best of me. Each thrust sent her to a higher level as we both climaxed. She trembled. I pulled out quickly.

Sweat beads formed on the bridge of her nose and forehead. I pulled her body close to mine. I put my head in between her breasts as she caressed the top of my head.

"Micah?"

"Yeah?"

"Should we be lying here, naked in one another's arms like we're lovers?"

"It's not such a bad idea. What do you think?"

She rubbed the top of my head. "We shouldn't. I think the liquor pushed you into doing this."

My hand softly touched her leg. I closed my eyes but then opened them to see her face. She wasn't being fair and she for damned sure wasn't seeing things from my side. I loved being her friend, but I wanted more. This was just the start of what I wanted to do to her.

"Do you think I'm too drunk to remember this in the morning?" I asked.

She threw the cover over her face. She was trying not to get too emotional or let the guilt take over. I snatched the cover off her face to see her teary eyes. She turned away from me.

"Look at me," I ordered. "Don't be a coward. I don't know what you think of yourself, but I love who you are. You're sexy to me."

When she didn't answer, I went into the bathroom. My thoughts were heavy. I needed a shower. Her low self-esteem was too much for me at that moment.

Cidnee

In my mind, I could see his dark naked body under the shower, and I was horny. I was too hot between my legs for things to get so technical. I eased out of his bed and entered the bathroom. He was already in the shower. I got in with him.

I wondered if the liquor had worn off and if he was feeling guilty for seducing me, but he questioned, "Why do you think that you're not attractive?"

"I'm sorry," I apologized putting my arms around him. "It's just hard for me to believe that you would like a girl that looks like me."

"Are you serious?"

"Yeah."

"Cidnee, I wish you were more confident in yourself. You're a beautiful woman."

"But, I'm not a fashion model's size."

"No, you're not, but so what? I've gotten to know you inside and out. You're so intelligent and that's sexy to me. Your insecurity can be a turn off at times."

"If you say so..."

He sighed and shook his head as he looked down at me.

I gave him a pout, poking my lips out.

He kissed my lips softly as if he couldn't resist staring at me.

I closed my eyes and enjoyed his kiss while my hands moved all over his tight body.

"Is this what you want Cidnee?" he nearly whispered in my ear.

"Yes," I whispered back as the steaming water beat down on us.

"You want me to suck you?"

I nodded, so he sucked my neck making his tongue swirl.

"You want me to give it to you?"

"Yes!"

He turned me around roughly, pushing me against the wall of the shower. He pressed his hardness up against me.

"Tell me what you want me to do," he demanded.

"I want you to have me, Micah."

"Is that all you want from me?"

"That's what I need right now..."

He slowly inched his way inside. He was nice, thick, and filling.

"Should I stop fucking you senseless?"

"I don't want you to stop."

"You don't?"

"No."

He rested against me, kissing the back of my neck. Then, he gave it to me deep and hard, the way I liked. I could feel him finally release. We stared at one another. That's when I realized my hair was soaking wet. That meant I was going to have to flat iron it before work.

I grabbed the soap and soaped up his towel. I washed him.

"What do you want me to do now?" I asked staring into his eyes.

"I want you to trust me."

I put my soapy hands around his neck. "You want me to just go with the flow?" I asked.

"Will you do that for me?"

I turned my back towards him, still in disbelief of what we were doing. He took the soap from me. He lathered the towel and gently cleansed my back. After washing one another, we both got out of the shower and wrapped clean white towels around our bodies.

"Micah..."

"Yeah?" He turned off the water.

"I'm cold."

He began massaging my shoulders letting his hands slip down into my towel. I moaned and dropped my shoulders.

"You have my feelings all over the place," I admitted.

He kept massaging, creating warmth with the palms of his hands. I closed my eyes while my breathing became heavier. Micah listened intently knowing just when to make the next move. He pulled me back to rest up against him. His hands went around my stomach and up to my breasts. The way he touched me, as if he couldn't feel those jelly rolls on my back and extra fat around me.

Micah

I leaned in and gave her my lips. She was happy to take them, hungrily. She sucked my tongue hard. I eased off the towel revealing all of her again, a sight I could never get sick of seeing. I grabbed her firmly, pulling her up against me tighter. Her eyes stayed locked on mine as she stroked me softly.

"Damn it," I nearly whispered. Her hands felt like butter, so soft and moist. I had one thing on my mind and that was to make her my love slave. "Get on your knees," I said in a deep commanding tone.

She looked me in the face as if she liked the idea of getting it on in our bathroom and she got on her hands and knees. She wiggled her butt a little. I played with her softly with the tip of me.

As soon as I was back inside of her, she turned to look at me with a look of pleasure all over her face.

I picked up my slow pace to a moderate rate. She took both fists full of the bathroom rug as I moved deeper into her. I had her by her stomach as she spread her legs as wide as they could go. I thrust deeper and deeper, harder and harder.

"Shit," she screamed. "Work me."

"You like that?" I asked.

"Yeah, get it baby..."

"You want me to get what?"

She managed to get out of my reach, bucking and kicking. She was on the edge of a big orgasm and she was trying to fight it.

"Where are you going?" I asked lifting her off the floor.

She screamed with delight as I carried her to her bedroom and tossed her on the bed.

"You can't run from me," I teased beating my chest like Tarzan.

She bit on her bottom lip moving her legs from side to side. She motioned for me to come back to her. I got on my knees positioning myself between her legs. She rubbed the top of my head as I kissed the inside of her thighs. She moaned lowly.

I made a trail to her hot spot and licked slowly. Her hands gripped my head. I made circles with my tongue against her clit. Her breathing increased and she moaned a little louder. This was my pussy.

"You better quit before we end up locked up in here all night," she whispered.

"That wouldn't be a problem would it?"

She laughed devilishly. "I'm not so sure just yet."

I pleased her until she squirmed. I chased her to the headboard and pinned her down. I didn't stop moving my tongue until she exploded.

"Why are you doing this to me?" she asked out of breath.

"What am I doing to you? Tell me. I want details."

"Micah, you're just something else," she replied biting her fingernail.

I entered her body again, this time showing no mercy. Each move was full of the passion that I couldn't disregard.

"Micah," she whispered in my ear, barely able to speak.

It was a sexy whisper, but I wanted a scream. Whispering was messing up my program. "What's that baby? You say something?"

"Oh Micah," she said a little louder.

I hit her spot deeper. I loved watching her sex face. I kissed her lips, swallowed her tongue. I lifted her legs high in the air.

"Micah!" she screamed. Her body began to shake again. "Micah! Micah! Micah!"

"Yes Cidnee," I answered her call with a smile coming to my face as I hit that target over and over.

"Micah!"

I gave her a few more hard pumps before I stopped again.

She looked at me in with disbelief all over her frown. "Can you go all night?"

"Hell yeah. I'm not done."

"Hell yeah, huh?" she asked giving my ear a taste with her tongue.

"You'll see."

She moaned kissing my ear, making her tongue flick back and forth. I got back inside of her, not to the pressure point yet, but just enough to have her lock those legs around me. I kissed her neck and continued to rock gently inside of her, but that feeling was coming on me.

I picked up the pace, took hold of her roughly, and I rocked her shit so good for another twenty minutes. She screamed out curse words asking God why. Her expression was sultry and sexy. My rhythm was set. Once in that mode, there was no stopping me. I hit her spot repeatedly and over again, making sure I got to that great pressure point that would send her over to the brink of pure madness.

Once I made her release some more mounting tension, she climbed on top of me. Her movements became like liquid as she bounced faster and faster. She didn't have the stamina of an unfit woman. She moved that ass. My fingers dug into her hips as I guided her ride. I felt myself losing my own train of thought. I was about to cum. We climaxed, once again, together. After we both let ourselves go, she collapsed on top of me.

Her sweaty body slid off and away from me. We lay on her bed listening to each other's quickened breath. I wondered what she was thinking. Did I go too far with her?

She didn't cuddle up next to me or whisper sweet things as if she loved me for giving her multiple orgasms. She faced the wall instead. I watched her back as it rose and fell. Because she didn't say anything, it made me question my performance.

"That was awesome," I heard her say as if she could read my mind.

"I agree."

"So what now Roomy?" she asked with curiosity.

I raised my eyebrow. If only she believed in my true intentions. This roommate situation was going to be taken to a whole new level. Keeping a secret this big from our friends was going to be tough, but for now, I was planning to get some rest and rock her shit again before work.

When Niyah Moore isn't writing, she's styling hair or taking care of her two young children. She has written, produced, and co-directed a few plays for her alumni Valley High School for the Advanced Theater class as a way of giving back to the community.

She has also written stories for *Mocha Chocolate: Taste A Piece of Ecstasy, Chocolat Historie D'Amour, Souls of My Young Sisters, and Crave: An Erotic Anthology.*

As divorced mother of two, Moore resides in Sacramento, California. She began writing at the tender age of nine, completed her first novel when she was twelve years old, and by the time she was sixteen she had completed three unpublished novels. She never gave up on her dream of becoming a published author and still shoots for the stars today.

Her debut novel **Bittersweet Exes** is available worldwide wherever books are sold. Niyah's sophomore novel **Even Better** will be released in 2011.

Point and Click Lover

by
Carla S. Pennington

I sat in front of my computer going back and forth over whether or not to agree to the terms and conditions of setting up a Black Planet account. I had heard so many stories from my girlfriends about how they all had met nice guys that some of my girlfriends were still with. I thought a few of my friends were like predators, looking for "Mr. Right Now" instead of "Mr. Right," and that seemed to work for them, as well. Whatever the case was going to be for me, I was ready to accept.

Nevertheless, I was afraid and skeptical about setting up the account. I knew there were sexual predators, rapists, and killers that lurked on such sites, but I knew I could also be talking to one of the same type of people sitting next to me in a club. There were stories on the news to remind me of these predators almost every day. I was tired of the same ole dating scenes and sitting at home doing nothing while my girls were out having fun with their point and click lovers. Their stories weren't helping the situation either. Listening to them brag about their wonderful dates or endless nights or weekends of undeniable sexual pleasure made me want to get in on some of the action, so I clicked the button to accept.

The very next day after signing up, I checked my account and felt like a giddy ass schoolgirl after seeing the numerous guys that had hit me up. There were so many to choose from that I spent the next few days ciphering through them. The straightforward ones turned me off immediately, especially with the line "When can we hook up?"

A few of them made me laugh at their words, but I wasn't falling for their weak ass lines either. Talking about how they can make my pussy wet, will make me scream, and shit like that. Hell, I could do that to myself.

The next three months after signing up, I made a few potential contacts, went out on a few dates that were fun, but nothing heavy. I found myself getting a little hooked and attached to the website. I was waking up in the middle of the night to check for messages.

On one particular morning, I was up around 2 a.m. checking my account. There was a lovely message left for me and it immediately caught my attention. He was neither trying to force anything nor was he being a desperate, blundering fool like some of the others had been. I jotted down the number that he left for me to contact him.

Later on that evening, he crossed my mind, so I took a few deep breaths before deciding to call his number. I eventually got my grown woman on and dialed.

"Hello, is Chris available?"

"This is he."

His deep, Chi-town accent shook my body.

"Hi, this is Reesa from Black Planet."

"Hey," he replied with much excitement in his voice. There was a bunch of racket going on in his background. "Reesa, can I reach you back at this number? I've got a lot going on around me now."

"Sure," I replied.

We ended our call. I didn't look at it as a loss or gain when he didn't call over the next few days, but during those days I came to grips that online dating just was not for me, so I cancelled my Black Planet account. I felt that being on there was a desperate move on my part to meet men and I really wasn't feeling it.

About a month or so after canceling my account, I received a call from a number I didn't recognize. I started not to answer, but my curiosity got the best of me.

"Hello?

"Reesa?"

"Who is this?" I asked without confirming if I was the person he asked for.

"Chris from Black Planet."

My mind began to wonder trying to place him, because I had put the whole Black Planet experience behind me.

"Chris, I am so sorry, but I don't remember you."

"Just think back. We talked briefly, because I had to rush off the phone and handle some business in my home.

It only took me a few seconds to remember him and when I did, I burst out laughing as I thought about the racket in his background.

"I'm sorry, Chris. How are you?"

"I'm okay. First, let me apologize to you for waiting so long to call you back. You may not believe this, but I wrote your number down that night and misplaced it. I just found it under a pile of papers at my computer desk."

"Sure you did," I replied sarcastically.

"I knew you wouldn't believe me, but it's the truth."

"So, now that you've found my number, where do we go from here?"

"You don't waste any time, do you?" he laughed.

"Time is too short to waste time."

"Well, you seem like an extremely interesting woman from the profile that I had to remember since you deleted it."

I couldn't hold in my laughter. We talked on the phone for hours and about two weeks later we decided to meet, especially since we found out that we were an hour's drive away from each other. He invited me to a party and I gladly accepted.

My butterflies rumbled and turned as I drove to the meeting spot. I was so nervous. Luckily, we pulled up at the same time. He had two of his female cousins in his SUV with him because he didn't know where he was going. We stepped out of our vehicles, stood, and stared at each other. What happened next made us realize that there was some type of connection between us. For some unknown reason, both of our car alarms began blaring. When we finally turned them off and regained our composure, we embraced each other. He smelled so damn scrumptious that I could have fallen asleep in his arms or jumped his bones for that matter.

We eventually made it to the party and had a blast. We danced all night, enjoying each other's company as if we had been dating for months. I hadn't danced in a while and when I danced with him, I felt as free as a bird. Then the DJ did the unthinkable. He played R. Kelly's *Imagine That*. I freaked Chris up and down that dance floor. All eyes were on me, even the DJ and the women's eyes. When the guitar solo came on, I vibrated and gyrated up, down, and all around Chris' growing bulge. All he could do was stand there and let me do my work. I needed to leave an impression when we parted ways later on and I did.

The next day he called and invited me to another party. I gladly accepted the invitation because I had so much fun the night before, but I remembered the drive home being a little awkward being that I was a little tipsy and tired. I assumed he knew that so he offered to get me a hotel room for the night. I was a little adamant at first until he informed me that the room was all mine and he had no intentions of staying. I accepted his invitation.

He paraded me around the party showing me off to his family and friends. They all quickly took a liking to me, especially the men. I guess it was my provocative dancing that drew them to me. I had to turn a few of them down mainly, because I didn't want my friend to feel disrespected and two, I still hadn't learned a lot about him. The party came to a close around 1 a.m. and Chris followed me to my hotel room.

"Well, I had a really nice time tonight," he said and after making sure that I made it to my room okay, he smiled showing off those deep-set dimples.

"So, did I. I haven't danced like that in years," I giggled.

"You could've fooled me and everyone else at the party. Girl, you've got some moves!" An awkward moment passed and he said, "Well, I'll stop by before check out time to see you off in the morning."

"W-Well, I was actually hoping that you'd wake up next to me before check out." I don't know what came over me, but I couldn't help myself. All I could think about was the fact that I hadn't been with a man in almost two years.

"That may not be such a good idea, Reesa."

"Why not?" I breathed as I stepped closer to him. "It is more than evident and so obvious that there is chemistry between us. I may have flunked the class, but I know about physical chemistry when I'm part of the mix."

"You've been drinking and I don't want you to feel like I took advantage of you."

"I had one drink and I am nowhere near drunk. Besides, if you won't take advantage of me then I guess I'll have to take advantage of you." I winked at him and before he could respond I grabbed him by his shirt and pulled him inside.

"Reesa...," he breathed heavily as I madly ripped open his shirt and attacked his neck and chest with my claws, lips, and tongue. "Reesa, come on now."

"I'm trying to, but you won't let me."

"I don't have any condoms."

"Don't worry about it. I have some," I replied and continued at my task.

"You came prepared, huh?"

"Always." I hungrily pushed him onto the bed and watched his body bounce when it hit the firm mattress.

"Reesa? Hmmmm, Reesa," he moaned as I licked all over his hairy chest and nipples.

I wanted him and wasn't afraid or ashamed to let him know just how bad. I straddled him and he squeezed my butt cheeks. In one swoop, he flipped me over onto the bed. He stood up and eagerly removed my shoes and tossed them across the room barely missing the television and lamp. I hurriedly unbuttoned my pants but saved him the honors of yanking them off. Seconds later, he freely and willingly shoved his tongue inside of me as if he had wanted to do so ever since we met. I latched onto his head and helped him out as he gripped my thighs and pushed my neatly shaven pussy further inside his mouth. I wrapped my legs around his neck and began grinding my hips and thrusting all over his face. Minutes later, I felt my walls contracting. He attempted to lift his head, but I quickly pushed it back down.

"Don't stop! Stay down there!" I said, panting and moaning. "Faster! Faster!"

He followed my orders and I was so happy that he did. A few seconds later, I exploded like an atom bomb.

"Where are the condoms?" he asked, anxious to enter me again.

"O-O-Over there," I breathed heavily as I pointed to my purse and squeezed my thighs tightly together.

I watched him eagerly dump the contents of my purse onto the table. Once he rummaged through the items and found the condoms, he hurried back to me discarding his pants and underwear in the process. He climbed on top of me and as soon as he entered me, I yelled to the top of my lungs.

"Reesa, baby, you have to be quiet," he whispered. "People are gonna think that I'm over here raping you."

Well, that's what it feels like, I said to myself.

"Am I hurting you?" he asked after watching me bite into a pillow.

I couldn't answer him. I was too busy focusing on what was going on between my thighs. His lips made their way to my breasts which intensified the moment even more for me.

"Don't be stingy with me," I spoke when I realized that he was holding back.

"What are you talking about, Reesa?"

"You're holding back from me."

"Baby, you are so tight. I can't give you all eleven of these inches right now."

"Well, when are you gonna give them to me? I've been waiting almost two years and..."

"And that's why I can't give them to you right now," he interrupted before slinging his tongue down my throat to shush me.

If I had to envision what heaven looked and felt like, I would say that I was experiencing it at that moment. He made my body feel like the precious temple that I knew that it was. He made me feel like I was the only girl that ever mattered to him. The way he caressed and made love to my body, mind, and spirit sent me to another level that I never knew existed, a state of euphoria. He touched me like he really wanted me, as if he wanted to learn every inch of my body. I wanted him to learn it too, because I wanted to learn his.

I maneuvered him onto his back knowing that I shouldn't have since he had informed me that he was packing eleven inches of what I knew was a damaging but pleasurable tool. I took a deep breath before I climbed on top of his mountain. I wanted to be a big girl and show him that I was a grown woman and that I could take whatever he dished out at me. It took me a few seconds to get it how I wanted it, but I did it.

"That's a high ass mountain, huh?" he smiled.

I said nothing because I was too busy focusing on the journey that I was taking. I let myself go and enjoyed the ride as he gripped my hips and squeezed my breasts.

"Chris, oh my God!" I cried out as he lifted and bounced me on top of him.

"You want it all, right?"

"Yes! Yes, I do! I can take it!"

He flipped me on all fours and mounted me from behind.

"I think you're gonna need this," he spoke after handing me a pillow to bite down on or yell into.

When he entered me, I screamed into the pillow. The pillow eventually wound up on the floor and before I knew it, I was hanging off the side of the bed clawing at the carpet. He kept pulling me back to him and my hands eventually were planted on the wall for leverage.

"Chris! Chris!"

"Is this what you expected, baby?" he asked as he leaned into me and kissed my earlobes. "Isn't this what you wanted?" he asked more aggressively after yanking my hair.

"Yes! Yes!"

He maneuvered my body against the headboard and ordered me to lift my arms up as high as they would go. I did. He kissed every inch of my neck, my back, my ass and then he went in for the kill. He slipped his head between my legs and ate me out. He clutched my butt cheeks so that I wouldn't try to get away. I wanted to collapse, but I didn't. I glanced down at him and saw him looking up at me with his leering eyes. It turned me on even more knowing that he was looking at me. I rode his tongue until my atom bomb exploded again. I expected him to move after I released, but he didn't. He continued to eat me out. He lay me down on the bed when he realized that my body was going limp, but he did not stop what he was doing. He was right, I didn't know what to expect once I pulled him inside my room. All I knew was that I wanted him. I needed to be freed. I needed these stored juices out of me and he made sure that all of my pipes burst.

He pulled me to the edge of the bed, stood up over me, tossed my legs over his shoulder and entered me again. Eleven inches of pure pleasure. And the next move that he pulled sent me into overdrive. He started licking and sticking, I didn't know which way I was coming or going. He had me that discombobulated. He did those lick-and-stick moves for almost five minutes and when he started humming and vibrating on my yum yum, I could no longer hold my composure. My body jerked like I was having a seizure. I think I may have even freaked him out. I felt like I was having two orgasms at once; vaginal and clitoral.

"Are you okay, Reesa?'

I didn't answer. I had made it to the pleasure land and I had him to thank for it. When he realized that I was okay, he entered me again, grabbed my hands and lifted my arms above my head. He kissed every inch of my face including my damn eyelids. He slowly made his way down to my neck, then my breasts. He pulled out of me and started fingering me so that he could taste the rest of my body. I was drifting off into ecstasy. My body began jerking again.

"Let me stop playing around with you," he smiled, "and give you what you want."

"You've given it to me, Chris," I breathed heavily.

"No, I haven't."

He lifted me off the bed and slammed me against the wall. My breasts rubbed against his chest as he drove his hammer deeper and deeper inside of me. The kissing was intense, as well as the touching and feeling. This man had skills and he was using them well. Our bodies were soaked with sweat. The curls in my hair had fallen. The fake tattoo on my breast was no more. He buried his face under my neck like and ostrich in the sand. I heard his muffled growls and grunts and knew that he was cumming. When he was done, he set me down and I collapsed on the floor. I watched him walk over to my purse's contents that he had scattered on the floor and rummaged for another condom.

"How do you feel about rug burns?" he smiled after changing out the condoms.

He wasn't done with me. He was prepared to wear my body out and I was prepared to let him.

At that very moment, I thought, *Black Planet.com, thank you for my point and click lover!*

Carla S. Pennington is an established author with no future plans of powering down her laptop. She was born and raised in Prichard, Alabama where she currently resides with her three children. In 2002, she received her Bachelor of Arts degree with a concentration in journalism from SpringHill College in Mobile, Alabama. After graduation, Carla decided not to pursue her career in journalism because her heart and mind was always set on writing fiction novels and short stories, something that she has been doing since she was a young girl.

In 2005, Carla published her first novel, **FLING**, with a local publishing company, KyteFlyte Productions (www.kyteflyte.com). In 2008, one of her short, erotic stories, *Cruisin'*, heated up the pages in the *Mocha Chocolate* anthology. She has completed her second, untitled novel and is foreseen to be released in 2010 through LifeChangingBooks (www.lifechangingbooks.net). In 2010, she will also contribute to other erotic anthologies that include *Chocolat Historie D'Amour, Mental Seduction 2* and a few others.

In 1996, Carla was diagnosed with Multiple Sclerosis (MS). Over the years, the disease has halted her, but she refuses to let it stop her. She is currently working on a number of other projects that she plans to have published in the near future. Email her at carlapennington@hotmail.com or find her online www.myspace.com/badoleputtytat www.facebook.com/carlapennington

Lemonade Freak
by
C. Nicole Pierce

Known in the hood for stunting hard and picking up the best of the best women around, Rex was called the "Lemonade Freak." Yellow was his favorite color, his favorite drink at the bar was Ciroc and Lemonade, and let's just say he liked his women thick with long hair, and high yellow. Most of his chicks were either video vixens or the equivalent in beauty. He wasn't tied down to one woman and didn't have any plan to settling down at any point in his life. Well, that was until he met the one chick that changed the game for him.

For a brotha with money, his reputation was far from being a "trick off" who paid for a little time with a lady. Instead, he was known for not doing much for the ladies besides taking them for a couple rounds in the bedroom. Most of his women were just proud to say they'd experienced a reign with the "Lemonade Freak." There were even best friends who weren't even mad at one another when they'd see each other's names on the yellow brick wall. In a secret room off of his walk-in closet in his bedroom, Rex had a yellow brick wall that was full of signatures of proud women who had been there and experienced a good lemonade freaking. For him it was an ego booster, but for the ladies signing this wall was an accomplishment. He lived by the motto of Lil Wayne's song, "Every Girl." He was convinced that someday he'd accomplish just what Wayne had wished for in the song – to give every girl in the world a chance to experience the Lemonade Freak. Of course, he meant the fine, yella girls that were built up right in all the right places. But again, that was all before he met Ivy.

Ivy was different from all of the women he'd been with before because they'd all approached him, for the most part. Mostly bragging about what they'd do to and for him, they'd hope that he'd choose them over the next chick. When he'd finally choose a girl, he'd say "tonight is your one and only lucky night," because he had a reputation of never doing the same chick twice, and the women did not seem to care.

However, this woman that he saw as he was walking into his jeweler to pick up another yellow diamond chain was also there to pick up a bracelet. Judging by the karats in the bracelet, Rex could tell right off the bat that she either she was a woman who had her own or she had a man that was spending major gwap on her. Just her standing there talking to the jeweler caught his attention in a way that no other woman of her stature had done. The fact that she appeared to know absolutely nothing about him and was not interested in finding out anything about him boggled his mind. He thought she might have been some type of high class chick that thought she was a little bit "too good" for him. She appeared to be the educated type. After doing a double take at her natural beauty, he made a note that she wasn't stacked like the women he dealt with on the regular, but realized she had the perfect little physique that suggested she worked out regularly

Walking up to stand beside her at the jewelers' counter, Rex said, "You know yellow diamonds are my favorite jewel." He then smiled at her, revealing his pearly whites – another thing that drove the ladies crazy. Of course, he could have sported the lemonade-colored teeth, but he took pride in his perfectly white teeth.

She quickly glanced back at him. Then, as if he hadn't said a word turned her attention back to the jeweler who had been assisting her and started discussing the piece that she was buying.

Being the type of guy who'd never met a woman that wasn't falling head and heels all over him, Rex immediately became turned on by her rejection. It was the kind of arousal that he had never had before. It wasn't that his pride was hurt, but he was able to recognize an equal in this mysterious woman. He decided move in a little closer to her until he was looking over her shoulder.

"I guess you'd call that "pink lemonade," he said making reference to the pink diamonds that alternated with the yellow ones on the bracelet she was looking at.

Completely annoyed, she snapped at him without even turning around to acknowledge him fully, "Must you insist on engaging in conversation with me when you clearly see your attention is unwanted!"

Sam, the jeweler, laughed at the woman's retort. He'd known both of them as his regular customers for quite some time and found it hilarious that a woman was finally rejecting Rex. He'd always secretly envied the attention Rex received on the regular from bumbling broads with no pride and lower self esteem.

"Dang Sam! I see you got a feisty one up in here today," Rex said with one eyebrow raised before letting out a hearty laugh. Not wanting to push his luck with the lady any further, he put his hands in the air and backed away saying, "I'm sorry, pretty girl. My bad."

He decided to leave, making a mental note to call Sam up later to get the info on this chick. She was definitely one tough cookie that he intended to break. Once in the parking lot, he noticed an iced pink CLS550 Coupe that was the identical match to his Canary Yellow Coupe. He'd only decided not to drive it that day, because he felt like dominating traffic in his Denali.

"Oh snap! It looks like 'lil mama has some good taste in cars, too." He said as he walked past her car and slowly headed to his SUV. He would have bet money that the pink car belonged to the feisty little woman inside the jewelry shop. Knowing he was a step closer to cracking her code and getting the girl, he smiled. Later that night he called Sam up to see what he could find out about her. He knew if all else failed, he could throw in a 'lil cash to get Sam to sing like a bird.

"What up Sam," he said with a slight chuckle. "You probably already know what I want, don't ya mane?"

"I'm sure I can guess," Sam replied while joining him laughing. "You want to know all about the young lady who put you in your place today. Am I correct?"

"For sure."

"Well, I can tell you now, don't waste your time. She's not going for a guy like you," he offered, obviously not realizing Rex was ready to take the challenge. Of course, Rex took the challenge and began to question Sam even further. By the end of the call, he knew that she'd just attained her masters degree from Howard University, went to the Super Fitness Gym, and was an heir to a very powerful man with a wealthy estate in upstate NY. This meant that she was more than likely a spoiled brat who turned out to be successful, as well. A bad combination for a guy like Rex.

There was nothing worse than a woman who grew up with a silver spoon in her mouth, had an inheritance, and still worked hard as if she has no other choice. Those were a total different kind of breed of independent women, which meant his stunting would not impress her one bit. Especially when she would more than likely would just guess how he made his money. *Hustlers don't stand a chance with a woman like Ivy,* he thought.

He'd finally convinced Sam to give up her name. Instead of being discouraged, he became determined to figure every thing out about Ivy there was to know.

His attraction to her was strange, because she was all of the things that he usually didn't like. She wasn't thick, she had a spunky short cut, and her skin was more of a butter pecan than yellow like most of the chicks he'd dealt with. She stood about five feet seven to his six feet three frame and her body was the perfect shape for a slim toned woman with an athletic build.

Thinking about her late into the night, he did something that he'd never had to do in all of his years of freaking. He reached his hands under his cover until they found his throbbing manhood and masturbated for hours, all the while thinking of her moving up and down on his shaft with her pretty mouth taking charge. Her unique smell held his senses hostage, as he felt like she was really in the bed with him rubbing his wanting flesh up against hers, driving him into a sexual frenzy. He had never smelled a fragrance as sweet as hers out of the hundreds of women that he'd been with.

Somewhat embarrassed that he was jacking off, he stopped halfway through getting his fourth nut and hopped in the shower before hitting the bed and passing out.

Like every other Saturday morning, Rex got up and went to the gym. Using the tip off from Sam, he decided to visit the gym in the downtown DC area that Ivy attended. Since his membership covered all of the Super Fitness gyms in the DMV area, he would be able to visit the new location with no problem.

Hoping to run into her, he decided to ride in his truck again. In case she'd caught a glimpse of his whip the previous day, he didn't want to seem too flashy. Just as he was pulling into the lot, he spotted her pink car pulling into a parking spot near the entrance. He smiled knowing that she too paid that extra gwap for the Platinum membership, which included priority parking and a few other perks. He pulled in next to her and hopped out the truck grabbing his bag in one motion.

"You know they say that the second time is a charm," he said with a huge grin hoping that she would correct him.

"I guess they told you wrong," a woman who got out of the passenger side said with attitude. Now, this woman was more of his type. She was light skinned with longer hair and a body that would put the baddest chick in the game to shame. Even with all of Ivy's friend's sexiness, his eyes were still on Ivy as she silently walked to the door as if, once again, she had not seen him.

Ignoring her rude brush off, he rushed ahead to hold the door open for the ladies. Ivy didn't say as much as "thank you" the entire time, nor did she look as if she wanted to say anything.

"Ivy, what's with you?" He asked, pulling her by the arm to stop her. He called her name as though they went way back to the block or something. "You weren't this quiet yesterday," he added to see if he could strike a reaction out of her.

What he didn't expect was to get a reaction out of her friend that he could easily see himself bending over a hotel bed and giving a hundred good thrusts of his magic stick.

"Ivy what the fuck is this nigga talkin' about? You know I'm the one who picks the dicks around here, so I know you ain't got me fucked up! Are you up here messing around with this dude?" the woman yelled out in the middle of the entrance where Ivy and Rex had stopped to have their spat.

Rex was both surprised and turned on at the same time. Apparently, Ivy was into chicks and this woman speaking up for her was her other half. Ivy rolled her eyes, yanked her arm away from his grasp, and kept walking into the gym without saying a word to either of them.

"I know you hear me talking to you!" The young lady yelled again, this time growing angrier by the minute. She started to walk after Ivy toward the cardio machine, but must have known that she would not get far with Ivy's stubbornness so detoured to the bike room. When she saw Rex walking toward the cardio machines to follow Ivy, she turned around and jumped in front of him stopping him in his tracks. "What was that 'lil comment all about?" she asked looking him dead in the eyes.

"Why don't you ask Ivy?" he said with a slight smirk of insinuation on his face. "I'm sure she will tell you all about it," he added trying his luck. He figured if he made her mad enough, he might, at least, get a reaction out of her. He then brushed past her and headed for the treadmill next to the one Ivy was on. She was walking vigorously on the treadmill as if she was trying to relieve a week's worth of stress. She looked completely annoyed with the world and he knew he was the root of her current frustration. Knowing that, he smirked and opted to run quietly alongside her. Her friend had stormed away into the cycling room, put on her headphones, and was riding her cycle like there was no tomorrow.

After about 20 minutes of running, Ivy finally turned to him. "Why did you pull that stunt out there?" she asked, trying to keep her cool. "I don't even know you and you pretended as if we have something going on. What's your purpose?" she added calmly though her eyes were firm and seriously searching for an answer.

She stared at him so long that she nearly had to look away for a brief second. Looking into his cute face softened her fury. His skin was flawless and his smile was a certified panty droppa', so yes, she had to look away before she melted right there on the treadmill.

"Well honestly, I'm not sure why I did it," he said with the same smirk he'd worn since he first spoke words to her. "There is definitely something about you that makes me act out of character, so I really would like to get to know you better. Is that your girlfriend back there?" He asked the question, although he knew the answer.

At this point, they were both in cool down mode and walking slowly on the treadmills. He was enjoying every moment of their conversation.

"I don't have a girlfriend. That's Tisha, my roommate. I like men, by the way, and so does she. We do engage in a few "homie lover" activities from time to time, but there's clearly no ring on my finger and when there is one there it'll be from a man," she revealed with a sense of irritation with her roommate in her voice. As her cool down was coming to an end, she grabbed a towel and sanitary spray and wiped down the handles on her treadmill.

"Tisha is very confused about our situation. She tries to run away every man that she feels has the qualities to cause me to settle down. Why she saw that in you? I'm not sure. She has nothing to worry about," she said finally cracking a slight smile.

Tisha walked over and hopped on the treadmill next to Rex, just as she did that Ivy walked off the treadmill and into the weight room. Rex took that as a cue to follow her making sure he looked back and winked at Tisha before exiting completely. He was letting Tisha know that he was about to take her woman. That made her anger level rise to the next level. She put her treadmill on one of the highest settings and began running as fast as she could. Sadly enough for her, neither of the people she was frustrated with were paying her any attention. Rex had his mind on scoring a date with Ivy before leaving the gym and Ivy had her mind on everything but the two of them.

Since charming was his middle name, Rex was able to get Ivy's digits by the time they left the gym. He made a point to get her number when they were standing in front of Tisha, because he had inkling that Ivy would give it to him out of spite of her. He was right.

She seemed annoyed at Tisha's jealousy and was proven to be the type to do something just to agitate someone when she walked over to the front desk where Tisha was standing and asked the attendant for a pen. Once she had the pen and one of the gym's business cards, she wrote the number down on the back of the card and handed it to Rex. He glanced at Tisha, smiled mischievously, and wished both ladies well before walking away.

"So you just act like what we have is nothing in public, huh?" Tisha yelled nearly in tears when Rex was out of ear shot. "I mean, I never heard of a DL chick, but I guess it's a first time for everything," she added rolling her neck as they walked out of the gym and toward the car together.

Tisha wasn't prepared for the slap that landed on her face. She stood there looking dumbfounded as passersby stopped and began to watch their encounter. Still in the parking lot looking stupid, she just stood there looking crazy as Ivy started the car.

"Are you going to get in, or what?" Ivy shouted, as if she could care less one way or the other.

As soon as Tisha got in the car, she wished she hadn't said a word, because Ivy let in to her.

"Let me explain something to you sweetheart, because apparently you are confused," Ivy started. "First off, I don't ever deny anything I do that pleasures me and, second of all, I told you that this was merely an experimental phase in my life that you are blessed to be a part of. You know good and well that I have every intention to marry a man and as many men that you sleep with you should be honored that I let you come near me. Stop acting like I'm the giver in this. You're the one that does all of the eating and I allow you to, remember? Please learn your position in my life before I take it away." Ivy snapped her eyes back to the bustling traffic before pulling out of the lot.

Tears streamed down Tisha's face, but she didn't protest. She knew everything Ivy said was true, but she had wished to make her realize that they were meant to be together. Even with Ivy saying the harsh words to her that knocked her confidence down a little bit, she still believed that Ivy would come around, eventually.

Later that night Ivy made plans to go out with Rex. She thought they didn't have to do anything special, but she wanted to punish Tisha for her antics earlier that day. She had to let her know that she was not the boss of her life. Ivy was her own *wo*man, not Tisha's man.

While she wasn't normally interested in dating much, she figured being wined and dined for a change would be a welcomed break from her normal routine. As she was getting dressed, Tisha walked into her room without knocking.

"What do you want Tisha?" Ivy said, looking from the mirror to her friend. She was still wearing her bath robe after soaking in a nice tub of scented bubbles for nearly an hour.

Without answering her question, Tisha approached her slowly inching up closely to her behind, began kissing her neck, and meticulously removed her robe.

At that very moment, Ivy wanted to refuse her. She wanted to turn around and give Tisha another tongue lashing for thinking she would be so easy to appease after the stunt she pulled at the gym. She wanted to pull her robe up off of the ground and cover her naked body. She wished she had the strength to do what her mind wanted, but her body had different plans. Girlfriend had a tongue that could beat any man that had ever touched Ivy's kitty.

Kissing each other feverishly, they made their way from the mirror to the bed. Once they lay in their bed of lust, Tisha kissed Ivy from the nape of her neck down to her breasts, planting seeds of love all over her wanting body. When she reached the mounds of joy that held passage to the spot she loved to taste, she spread Ivy's legs and ran her tongue up and down each thigh. Once Ivy had all of the foreplay that she could take without begging for her tongue, Tisha began doing what she did best and provided Ivy with orgasm after orgasm from the pleasures of her tongue. Once her bulb was so swollen that it was about to burst, Tisha sucked it gently until the nectar came flowing onto her tongue. Ivy bucked about on the bed rotating her pelvis to meet the lashes of Tisha's tongue. She pulled Tisha's curls as she moaned loud enough to piss the neighbors off. As a finale to their passionate tryst, she maneuvered her tongue roughly over Ivy's tugged out bulb in an act to let her know whose pussy Ivy had attached to her body. She kissed both of Ivy's thighs and walked out of the room closing the door behind her without saying a word leaving Ivy completely spent.

It was strange, but Tisha got off from doing things like that. She wasn't a full blown lesbian, because she preferred dick over pussy, but it was something about the taste and joy of pleasing her roommate that kept her coming back for more.

Ivy hopped back in the shower to wash away the remnants of Tisha from her body and decided on a slinky black dress that accented her curves very well to wear on her date with Rex.

"I'm headed on a date with one of the sexiest men alive and I'm going to love every moment of it," she said to herself as she put on her signature fragrance that had to have been made especially for her, because it matched so well with her skin.

Her cell phone rang flashing Rex's name across the screen, so she grabbed her purse and keys and headed out the door.

Meanwhile back in her bedroom, Tisha had other plans. She'd sat on the couch smirking at the possibility of Rex coming over after his date with Ivy and the three of them engaging in a little ménage trios. She'd peeped him at the gym and deep down inside she was more angry that she hadn't spotted him first than she was about Ivy dating him. Everything about him was a turn on and she had it in her mind that she wanted to turn him out. If Ivy wasn't willing to share him, she'd simply have to take him away from her.

"Hmmm, little girl, you don't know what you're up against. Either share it or get it took," she said to herself laughing maniacally and then popped in a good porn DVD to get herself ready for Ivy and Rex's return home.

"Where are we going," Ivy asked growing increasingly impatient that they'd been driving around for almost thirty minutes without any inkling about where they were headed.

"Be patient, baby girl. We will get there soon. I like to take the scenic route when I go out with someone special, which isn't that often," he replied. It wasn't exactly a lie because he didn't take women out much and when he did it was mainly to a lounge or bar to warm them up for a night of sexual aerobics. Rex had decided to drive his car that matched hers, so that she'd see they had similar taste. To his surprise, that prominent detail didn't seem to strike the tiniest of response from her. Instead, she was focused on where they were going and why it was taking so long.

"You aren't in a rush to get back home to the wifey, are you?" he asked jokingly noticing immediately that it struck a nerve. Not only did she not respond to him, but she rolled her eyes, as well. He made a mental note to lay off of the lesbian jokes. He'd been with plenty of women and taken part in several threesomes, but this woman he wanted all to himself.

Their long drive ended at a nice little quaint restaurant near Baltimore on the Harbor. They both enjoyed the food. It turned out that she loved seafood just as much as he did. Many jokes came to his mind, but he decided against cracking them since they were having such a great time. After dinner, they ended up at a small upscale lounge to have a few drinks.

During the drive back home, he'd made it up in his mind that he was going to decline if she invited him upstairs. Although he couldn't realistically see himself telling her no if she licked her bronze lip gloss covered lips one more time like she had been doing all evening, he was falling for her fast and he wanted to show her some respect by keeping it moving. The night went very well and he could clearly see that she was feeling him more than he'd expected. It could have been the liquor, but he had no problem blaming it on the goose if it meant he ended up putting it on her, but he was going to attempt to restrain and not take it there on their first date.

When they pulled up to her condo, they had a moment of taking each other in completely before she leaned in to passionately kiss him. Even though the kiss was unexpected, he leaned to take full advantage of her soft and full lips. They paused long enough to gaze into each other's eyes before locking lips for another kiss.

"I think we should take this upstairs," she said breathing deeply after coming up for air. She wanted to see if he could match the fever of his kisses in her bed. She knew that if she could found a man that could kiss the kitty better than Tisha she'd be able to close the lesbian chapter of her life. At that very moment, Rex gave her hope in his kiss that he had what it took to go ahead and slam that book shut!

Her relationship with Tisha only began because they'd been roommates for so long that they were comfortable enough walking around and sleeping in their underwear. One night, Ivy was stressed out. It had been a long week of finals and she had spent many long hours studying and working. It was no secret that Tisha liked to dabble with the female anatomy, but when Ivy fell asleep that night Tisha decided to help her relieve some stress. Ivy woke up moaning and thrusting her pelvis to the best oral sexual experience she'd ever had in her entire life. Although it seemed weird at first to see her best friend and roommate between her legs providing her this pleasure, she relaxed and allowed Tisha to spontaneously give her body what it needed. There was not a man she'd ever met who could give her that kind of satisfaction.

"Are you sure you want to take this upstairs?" Rex asked incredulously, turning off his ignition.

"One hundred percent sure," Ivy said, smiling mischievously and once again running her tongue over her soft lips.

"If that's true, then what were you just thinking about?"

"Oh, nothing. Well, maybe something like pouring whipped cream all over you and having you for my breakfast in the morning."

With that said, Rex hopped out of the car and ran around to open her door. He had completely forgotten about his pact with himself to decline her offer.

While walking upstairs, he had so many thoughts that crossed his mind. He was ready to put his award-winning bedroom skills to use on her and if she was meant to be his lady then the fact that they slept together on their first date wouldn't get in the way, now would it?

When they walked through the door, Tisha was spread out on the couch wearing nothing but her panties. Instead of covering herself with her blanket, she eyed them with a knowing look as they walked to Ivy's bedroom. When she heard the bedroom door lock, she caught an instant attitude and wanted to barge in the room behind them, but they had a system. Whenever one of them locked their bedroom door it meant the guy was off limits and wasn't share worthy.

Ivy didn't really bring guys home and she never took Tisha up on the offer of a threesome with any of the guys she did bring home, but Tisha was really hoping that this guy would be up for grabs. She really just wanted him to see how much better she was at oral sex than he was and, of course, she wanted to feel his pipe inside of her. Instead of receiving any of the three-play she was expecting for the night, she pulled her Mandingo-sized vibrator out of her stash inside of the coffee table and positioned herself to lay on the floor across from Ivy's room. She completely undressed herself removing her panties and bra and proceeded to please herself with the vibrator. She hoped either they'd hear her pleasuring herself and ask her to join, or she'd get off by hearing their sounds of lovemaking.

On the other side of the door, Rex planted kisses all over Ivy's body. He began at her forehead and slowly worked his way down to her thighs. Once he reached the heat between her thighs, he slowly spread her legs apart and began to gently plant kisses on her pantiless kitty. *She's beautiful, sexy, smart, sassy, and doesn't wear panties. What more can a brother ask for?* he thought as he slowly massaged her thighs with his hands and worked his tongue over her heated center.

He wanted her to get the full effect of his sensual tongue action. He could tell that she was enjoying it as much as he was when her juices began to flow into his mouth, as she came over and over and over in a matter of minutes. Multiple orgasms flowed from her sensitive bulb as she moaned and called his name awaiting the next trip to ecstasy.

Her entire body yearned for more and he was more than ready to give her the kind of love that she needed. The kind that her roommate could not give her in one thousand years. He was ready to insert himself vigorously into her tight body.

However, she had different plans. She lifted his head and kissed him gently as she sat up on the bed. Taking control of the situation, she stood and gently pushed him onto his back on the bed. Planting sweet kisses on his body until she reached his manhood, she slowly took him into her mouth and began working her tongue up and down with no hands. She kept a circular motion going until she was able to put his entire girth and length in her mouth. It was not long before his cum gushed out and instead of rejecting his juices she let each warm drop slide down her throat.

At that point he knew he was in love. Sure women had swallowed him before, but none as graceful and ladylike as she had and absolutely no woman meant what she meant to him on a first time. The loving look he gave her as she mounted him and began to rock in a motion that he was unfamiliar with was a look that he was not used to. He caught her rhythm and began to rock her back.

"Ivy, I...girl I..." He stopped in the middle of his sentences when he heard sounds that were coming from the hallway. "Is that what I think it is?"

Ivy shook her head in disbelief. "It definitely is."

They both laughed and slipped back into their private world of creating the best passionate moments they'd ever experienced. Little did Tisha know, Ivy and Rex were so deep into their love making that nothing she did could break the concentration in that room. Plus, they both knew that she just wanted some attention, too. After switching positions and climaxing time and time again, the two finally fell asleep holding each another tight as if neither wanted to let go.

By the sound of things, Tisha knew that this man had the business and she was determined to find out more about him and what he did for a living. She knew the best way to get rid of him was to expose him to Ivy. She went into her room and fell asleep plotting to find out as much as she could about him as soon as possible. The next morning she came out of her room to find Rex and Ivy sitting at the dining room eating breakfast.

"Oh, so you fixed breakfast for him, I see," she said with jealousy almost burning her tongue as the words fierily left her mouth.

"Yes, I think there is a little left on the counter," Ivy said. She was so engrossed in Rex, she did not even look up at Tisha when she spoke to her.

They both were wearing robes and Ivy was confused as to where his came from, but she wasn't about to ask any questions.

"No thanks. I have something important to do this morning," Tisha said, leaving out of the house slamming the door behind her. Even more upset after seeing the glow in both of their eyes at the breakfast table, she stormed outside and proceeded to slash Rex's tires before jumping in her Toyota Camry and speeding out of the drive way. She wanted to make it look as if one of his crazy girlfriends had found his car and slashed his tires. This would be only the first of many tricks Trisha would pull. Laughing as she drove down through a busy intersection, she said, "I'm going to make this lemonade freak wish he never met us."

My name is Nicole and I'm an entertainment publicist and author in Chicago. Most people may know me as **C. Nicole the PR Girl**. I've been working within the industry for a short while, but have managed to meet some great people along my journey. My ambition has caused me to build some very beneficial relationships while setting the foundation for my career. I love to surround myself with creativity. I've been in the workforce since the age of 14 and realized early on that a 9 to 5 wasn't for me. I'm very determined to succeed in the entertainment industry and possibly become the next female mogul. I'm taking everything one step at a time while making my mark on the world, one city at a time. Aside from the wonderful world of publicity, promotions and booking, I'm also a published author. I've been published in two separate anthologies *Mocha Chocolate: Taste A Piece of Ecstasy* was released March 29, 2008 by Nayberry Publications. The second, *"Don't Trip"* is an urban anthology published by Aldridge Publishing that is yet to be released.

If the name C. Nicole or PR Girl doesn't ring a bell to you now, keep listening because the bells shall be ringing loudly in due time. I can be found online at www.cnicoletheprgirl.com or reached at cnicolepr@gmail.com.

Marco Polo by Lovelle

"Oooh, it's nice and warm," Kimora stated as she dipped her sexy pedicured feet into the Jacuzzi causing the water to make a ripple effect across the surface. As she lowered her hypnotizing body deeper into the liquid relaxer, my dick couldn't help but get hard looking at her curvy, toned, voluptuous, caramel body. Wearing a red bikini top that barely covered her full, perky C-cup breasts, but fully exposed her flat toned tummy and a low-cut bikini thong bottom that clearly showed that she waxed downstairs already had me prematurely ejaculating. To call her sexy would have been an understatement. Kimora was more than gorgeous, she was absolutely stunning. Long, natural, jet black, silky, and thick hair that swayed past her pierced belly button, hazel green chinky eyes, and cute little button nose were inherited from her Cambodian mother. Full luscious lips, wide voluptuous, "baby making" hips, and a well-proportioned ass suitable for any brotha were all passed down from her father's African-American genes. Kimora had that smooth, radiant skin that every woman envied and a sexy exotic look that made her simply irresistible to any human being. Flat stomach, toned thighs, charming dimpled smile...she could have possibly made Viagra go into inexistence.

"Why are you sitting so far away? I don't bite." I smiled then licked my lips at her. She shyly smiled, showing those seductive dimples of hers, then scooted her mesmerizing body closer to mine.

"Better?" she asked so close to me that I could still smell the Pinot Grigio wine we had at dinner earlier lingering in the air from her sweet breath.

"Much better." I said coolly, not wasting any time as I went for the kill. Leaning forward while holding her chin, I kissed her softly and then let my tongue part her luscious lips and explore the inside of her moist mouth. I sensed a little hesitation from her end, so I naturally became more aggressive, sliding my free hand down to her crouch area. Hey what could I say, I was a man. It was naturally in my DNA to take the initiative.

"Mmmm, wait a minute," she stated as if we were moving too fast. She pushed me off of her then looked dead into my eyes, so innocently.

"What's wrong?" I asked, caught off guard and also slightly offended.

"I'm sorry, but this is moving a little too fast," she stated.

I smirked to myself as I shook my head; sometimes I could be a great mind reader, but then again most women could also be so predictable at times such as this.

"How so?" I exhaled deeply, grabbing my champagne flute that was sitting behind me on the cement deck and downing the rest of my substance rather quickly. I really didn't have time for this hard to get shit. I thought we were already past that stage. Here I was, this very handsome, very established, well-groomed, well-endowed black man with his shit together. I was about six foot three, one hundred and ninety pounds solid, nice muscular build, smooth dark chocolate complexion, neatly maintained dreads hanging a little past my shoulder blades, dark brown bedroom eyes, charming smile, a few tattoos from when I was in the service years ago, neatly trimmed mustache and goatee, and a dick the length and width of a cardboard paper towel roll. Not to mention, I had my own three-bedroom/two-bathroom house with a spacious backyard for family and social gatherings, two sports cars, and a motorcycle, plus a very well paying job. I was perfectly capable of being with any woman I desired, and in some cases there were women who would immediately drop down to their knees and give me amazing head the minute I said "Becky." Instead I was sitting next to a half fried chicken/half cat eating ass mutha fucka who couldn't appreciate a good black man and what he had to offer.

"One minute we're enjoying a lovely candlelit dinner and the next minute you're trying to stick your tongue down my throat," she explained, attempting to try and persuade me that we should take things slow and not rush into it.

Spare me, I thought. She acted as though she had never gotten down and dirty on the first night with those rough neck hoodlums she was used to dealing with on a regular basis at various music video shoots. Or never given celebrities "special treatment" up in the VIP section when she had to be a hostess at big superstar events. She was one of those video vixens that didn't mind exploiting her body for the world to see but acted all sadity and snooty behind the cameras. Obviously, those no-talented rappers filled her head up with pure bullshit, because my good looks alone was going to break her out of that mold and I would be up inside of her in no time.

"Well, I'm sorry, but the opportunity presented itself. With all due respect, I brought you here because I enjoy your company and thought you were a woman ready to take on a few adventures with me, not some lil' girl afraid to experience life and live in the moment. We've been dating for a while now, so excuse me if I find you incredibly beautiful and completely irresistible, especially wearing that sexy ass Ed Hardy bikini."

She smiled, so I eyed her seductively licking my lips then continued. "Do you honestly expect for my dick *not* to get hard looking at you right now? Come on now, I get turned on just by the sound of your sweet angelic voice so just imagine how I'm feeling at this very moment." She turned red immediately. I thought that was sexy. "Honestly, are you really that shy, Kim?" I asked.

"No," she truthfully answered, shocking the hell out of me.

"Then prove it," I stated with a sly grin.

Her left eyebrow arched up like she was about to do some mischievous activities. She stretched out her arms then reached behind her back, fondling with her bikini top strings as I sat back, enjoying the pressure coming from my Jacuzzi turbo jets.

With one quick motion, Kimora's top fell into the water. My heart skipped a beat and my dick developed a pulse of its own as I caught a glimpse for the first time of Kimora's perky breasts in full, uncensored view. Caramel honey surrounding milk chocolate pearls. My dick was getting harder by the second and I just couldn't compose myself. *Hey what can I say, the girl was sexy.*

I quickly soared through the water to get to her body and attempted to suck on her erect nipples, but she gently pushed my chest then quickly floated back.

"No, no, no..." she smiled as she shook her manicured pointer finger at me while her other arm covered her breasts. I hated to be teased. "Close your eyes," she purred with the prowess of a bobcat.

I inhaled deeply then exhaled loudly as I willingly obeyed. I listened closely, but I was only able to hear the sound of water dripping into the Jacuzzi. Then I felt the warmth of the material from her bathing suit on my face. I could feel her soft wet hands adjusting the breast part of the bikini top over my eyes then tying the strings tightly around the back of my head.

"What are you doing?" I smiled, curious to know what she had planned. Deep inside, I knew she was a little freak. I felt her quickly move away from me as the waves she created rocked my body and caused my dreads to sway a little.

"Polo!" she yelled, then giggled.

Ahhh...so she wants to play, I thought to myself as I grinned devilishly then licked my lips. If she wanted to play little water sports games so I could get to that sweet creamy center of hers, then I was all in.

"Marco," I said coolly as I stretched my arms out in front of me, walking blindly through the water to her sweet voice.

"Polo..." she tried to whisper, but I could hear her clearly to my left. With one quick motion, I leaped my body as far as it would allow me in the water and I was able to capture her tender body in my arms. *Paranoia has its advantages.*

I held her in my muscular arms tight and then on her very own, she passionately kissed me. Her damp arms wrapped around the back of my neck underneath my brother locks as the water from her hands dripped down the middle of my back. We got more into the kiss as our lips smacked, tongues got entangled, and moans escaped from both ends. My rock hard dick was pressed firmly against her lower abdomen through my swimming trunks as my hands slowly moved towards the back of her head, my fingertips gently caressing her scalp. Transferring my kisses to her graceful neck and earlobes as she squirmed out of pleasure, I could feel the obvious heat coming from both of our bodies. We didn't need the Jacuzzi's warmth on this cool night. I sensed she was still a little tense so to relax her a little more and put her mind at ease, I decided to continue the game that she had started.

"Mmmm...Marco," I said sexually in my low tenor voice as I created a passion mark on her smooth creamy skin.

"Polo." She giggled and then moaned.

I took that as a sign to go lower, so I cupped her left breast gently and began flicking my tongue on her protruding nipple, making it even more erect than it already was. Pulling her nipple inside of my mouth with my moist lips, I began to suck on them as if I expected for something to come out. Nibbling then biting softly on them had her rubbing all over my dreads, gathering them up in her hands and clinching them tightly through her fingers. That turned me on!

After about four minutes of attention to both succulent breasts, I decided to show some love to her sexy ass stomach, kissing all over her ribcage, slowly licking all the way around her belly button, and sucking her dangling belly jewelry in my mouth. As my tongue swirled around the inside of her deep cave (she had an inney), I could hear her inhaling deeply through clinched teeth as her fingernails grazed my back a little. I loved the sound and feel of her.

"Does that feel good baby?" I asked in my most sexy voice, while nibbling at her navel.

"Mmmm... polo, polo, polo," escaped her luscious lips.

I smirked to myself as I debated on getting really freaky. Thinking with my *lower head*, I swiftly removed her bikini top from my face letting it fall into the water, inhaled deeply, and then lowered my entire body down into the warm water. I began to adjust the crotch of her bikini bottom, pushing it just enough to the side so I could begin eating the shit out of her sweet pussy. I flicked my hurricane tongue hard and fast against her phat clit, giving it that vibrator effect as I spread her legs further apart with my shoulders so I could really get in there. With one quick motion, I vigorously pulled the strings unloose on her bikini bottom and watched it slowly sink to the floor of the Jacuzzi tub. With both hands, I grabbed the back of her toned thighs, pushing them up as her entire body lifted out of the water so that I could slide my vicious tongue inside of her wet opening. Her legs automatically clamped my head between her thighs so at times it was difficult to come up for air, but I was pretty good at holding my breath for an extended period of time so it was all good. I was a pussy-eating monster, determined to make her cum. I sucked on her clit with just enough force to send her entire body into sexual shock. Her legs began to tremble, so I came up for air just in time to witness her trying to grip anything that she could get her hands on to keep from moaning loud enough to disturb my neighbors. The powerful orgasm took over her body for the moment. Her eyes were shut tight. Her straight white teeth bit down firmly on her plump juicy lips and my right hand continued to play with her swollen clit. Her body continued to jerk, even after the orgasm had subsided. I smiled and went back underwater to eat some more.

The last time I came up. I didn't give her any warning. My throbbing hard dick eased right up inside of her tight wet pussy. She gasped taking in my size, gripping my arms tightly as I filled her up nicely. A good four inches still attempting to make its way in with each fulfilling stroke. I could tell she had "been around" because my dick had never slid up that far inside of a woman that quickly without me properly breaking her in, usually I could barely get the head in without clever maneuvering. Kimora was still nice and tight, even though she had a few miles on her.

I continued to ram my dick inside of her with a passion like tonight was the last time I would fuck. I wanted to ram all of me inside of her that she allowed me to. Once she got a hang of the rhythm, she wrapped her firm athletic legs around my waist. That shit sent me into overdrive. My hands grabbed her juicy apple bottom ass firmly and I pounded away inside of her. The sound of the water splashing every time her phat ass slammed down on my dick was exhilarating, but her sweet voice barely uttering "Fuuuck..."was almost enough to make me bust a nut right inside of her.

Instead, I lowered her back down into the water and said, "Mmmmm. Go grab a towel from the lounge chair and get in doggy style top of it."

Ready to oblige, she positioned herself on the edge of the Jacuzzi. Her sexy pedicured feet almost touching the surface of the water. Oh, what a beautiful sight of her round, plump ass sticking straight up in the air! It automatically had my dick standing at attention. Not able to wait another second without contact, I dove into that pussy once again tongue first, still standing in the water. I just loved the way her juices tasted and I loved the fact that she had a big phat clit, too. I could suck on that juicy muthafucka all day long. I sucked and nibbled on her clit and slid my finger inside of her still tight wet opening as I attempted to find her g-spot.

After a few flicks and jolts, with my middle finger still planted deeply inside of her, she came all over my tongue. *"My, my, a squirter,"* I thought. If that was not a major turn on, then I don't know what was. After every drop of her sweetness was swallowed, I lifted the bottom half of my body from the water and I positioned myself behind her. I smacked her right ass cheek and it jiggled like Jell-O.

She moaned.

"You like that?" I asked as I smacked the left side.

"Polo..." she confessed.

I got up from the ground then hurried and ran over to the

patio table. I grabbed my wallet and retrieving a Magnum condom. I didn't know what I was thinking when I slid inside of her unprotected the first time. I never went raw and this sexy ass, promiscuous, video vixen was definitely not an exception.

I quickly slid the barrier on, safely secured it, and walked back over to the Jacuzzi where she was still patiently waiting for me in the doggy-style position. I got back down on my knees, scooting much closer to her body than I had been before. I held on to her hips and kissed up her spine to the nape of her neck. She quivered from anticipation.

"I'm about to tear this pussy up," I whispered in her ear. Before she even had the opportunity to respond back, I shoved my dick so far and hard inside of her you would've sworn my shit was going to come straight out of her throat. She jumped and screamed in ecstasy, gripping the hell out of the towel and then started backing that ass up on this dick. Her pussy was so wet, tight and warm; *perfect combo.* I knew I was going to nut soon, so I decided to go ahead and get buck wild before I came as I grabbed a handful of her silky wet hair, arched her back to the point where her stomach was touching the towel, and pumped in and out of her fast as hell, still smacking her ass cheeks rough until they turned red and had handprints on them

"Ugh ugh ughhhh..." she screamed as she tightened her pussy muscles around my dick and her body went into multiple convulsions; her way of letting me know that this dick was doing her body more than good. The sound of her cumming and the feeling of her pussy walls contracting around my dick did it for me. I hurried and pulled out of her, ripping off the condom right away and jerking off my dick fast as hell until I skeeted all over her ass and back. I was moaning so loud, barely able to keep my composure.

After every drop of cum had fallen, I collapsed back into the warm Jacuzzi, falling deep into the water. I then came back up almost instantly. Dick still semi hard, floating atop the water with my arms stretched wide, breathing heavily and in a complete daze. If I smoked, I would have definitely been in need of a nice cancer stick or joint at that moment.

As I lay there trying to gather my thoughts, there was really only one word that came to mind that would have been most appropriate for that moment in time. "Marco." I exhaled. I heard Kimora giggle as she still remained in doggy style position, face down and ass up.

Then she called out to me. "Polo."

Lovelle started her writing career at an early age. Being the youngest and only girl out of four children, she developed a very unique imagination and also a love for reading and writing. While she was still in elementary school, she wrote and illustrated her first children's book Beware of the Bean Burrito, which was featured in the local newspaper. She wrote her first novel, Alize, on the Rocks her junior year of high school and was later published in 2006. It was then that she discovered her passion for writing Hip Hop/Urban Erotica Fiction. Also in 2006, she began writing Urban Erotica short stories and hustling them in the local urban community.

Raw & Uncut: The Street Erotic Anthology is her 2nd published manuscript. She also contributed her short story *A Hell of a Hard Drive* to LadyElle Publishing's *Chocolat Historie D'Amour* Anthology. Lovelle currently resides in Florida, where she is working on her next novel.

"When I was younger, I can still remember to this day, people used to ask me what I wanted to be when I grew up. Most children said a doctor, lawyer, even an astronaut. But, I was always different. I was proud to say that I wanted to be an author and I am even more proud to say that I've accomplished what I've wanted out of life. Many people can't say that. I'm doing what I always wanted to do. I'm being what I always wanted to be. Does it get any better than that?"

- *Lovelle*

Engine Trouble by Luscious Lynn

There really should be some sort of shame on it all, but I must admit that I have a serious addiction to sexy male exotic dancers. Honest, I do! While this addiction is both pitiful and shameful, what can I say? Hell, spank me! The male dancers in the Chicago area have had a history of driving me into a sexual craze and I don't see the future changing any time soon. There are even three out-of-town dancers that I adore, as well. I adore them more than cooked food and *that* is a stretch for me, I do declare. I believe that if I had a dick like a man those gorgeous hunks standing next to me would literally get my dick hard. The sad thing is that every couple of months I get a new crush on a different dancer, but of course, a girl still has her favorites. Truth be told, I've had some pretty steamy encounters with some of them. Some encounters so nice that they would make the hairs on the back of your neck ripple, so what I tell you next, well it's a true story.

One Friday night, my crazy friend and I were at an all-male stripper lockdown party having a great ass time watching one sexy chocolate stallion after another do their thing. One of my favorites, at least my favorite that particular night, was looking more delicious than a yummy piece of chocolate fresh out of the box and dripping in honey. He gyrated feverishly to the music giving me a show. From the moment we'd laid eyes on each other, we could not focus on anything else in the room. I could not keep my eyes off of him, and well he seemed to be caught up staring into my gaze.

Even with my newfound skinny body, I was still a little

shy. I had lost so much weight over the past months that I was getting hella attention from men, and it was a bit new to me. Don't get me wrong, I felt worthy of the attention and there wasn't a damn thing wrong with my self esteem, but I was kind of apprehensive about being the aggressor and instigating a fling.

As lust filled the air, time was sliding by. It was starting to get late, so Jessica turned to me and said, "I've got to get home, so I can get a few hours of shut eye before work tomorrow."

Knowing that my friend only came out because I wanted to get out of the house tonight and knowing that she had work tomorrow, I reluctantly guzzled down the rest of my drink and said, "Sure. Let me finish up this drink and we can leave." I, too, decided that we had had just about enough of watching dicks swinging for one night, but my, my, my the one chocolate brother that I kept connecting with was really turning me on. Maybe it was just as well that we got out of there, so I could go somewhere and cool off. Whew!

Gathering our purses and coats, we said goodbye to a couple of our girls and headed for the nearest exit. Tanya, Tamara, Tee, Brenda, and a few others said, "Bye," as we exited, but remained seated with their attention fully focused on the men in the room. Those chicks didn't look like they planned on leaving no time soon. They were going to see if they could score a freelance lover for the night and hey, I wasn't mad at them. Once we got outside in the cool night air, Jessica and I were giggling, singing, dancing, and cracking up like two alkies in a pod. The alcohol had us feeling some kind of nice, so we were acting really stupid as we walked towards where my car was parked. We reached the car and got in. I put the key in the ignition and turned. The piece of shit wouldn't turn over.

"Girl, I don't know what could be wrong this time. If it isn't one thing it is another with this car. I just got it out of the shop yesterday." I hit the steering wheel, pissed because, for one, I had just had the car fixed the day before and two I remembered the mechanic told me I had to hit the wat-zik that was connected to my thingy stick with my shoe a few times to get it to crank when it acted up on me. Three, I was tired as hell and didn't feel like playing with a half broke car and hell, I had on new stilettos, to boot. Hitting parts of my engine with my stiletto was out of the question.

"I guess, I'll be going to work with no sleep after all," Jessica said, sounding exasperated after we tried unsuccessfully to get the car started by hitting it with my stiletto.

Defeated, we just got out the car and leaned against it, looking around like two lost puppies. Outside was desolate, except a few cars passing up and down the highway that ran in front of the club. Everybody was still inside getting their party on in the warmth of the club and fulfilling their most lustful desires, if only in their minds.

We were just about to give up on the hope of getting home any time soon and go back into the club to at least enjoy the rest of the show when, *oh my GOD, Mr. Oooou DAMN*, walked around the coroner.

I was the first one to see him. He looked as if he were looking for someone in particular. It thought that maybe he had some kind of hookup outside of the club that he was waiting on, but before I could think much more about his situation my big-mouthed girlfriend had hunched up against me and said, "Girl, he is fine ass! Call his sexy ass over here right quick, so he can help us out."

She winked at me as if she had more on her mind than getting the car started. I thought she had wanted to get her butt home so that she could get some rest for work, but my first thought after hearing her suggestion was "oh, oh." Whenever Jessica suggested a move like that, nothing but trouble followed it.

I shook my head vigorously. "Naw, girl. I ain't calling him over here to help us. He probably doesn't know any more about fixing this car that we do; besides, I don't know what to say to him, anyway."

Realizing that I wasn't going to call the sexy chocolate stripper from the club over, she cut me off and screamed, "HEY! MR. OOOUDAMN! Can you come over here for a second?"

To add to my embarrassment, she was waving at him like she was attempting to land a plane. "COME ON OVER HERE AND HELP US!"

By this time, she was screaming like someone was trying to jack us for the raggedy car. I was too shame. I just placed my head in my hands and closed my eyes.

"No, you didn't." I wanted to scream the words, but I whispered them to her through closed teeth as he looked in our direction and gave a sigh of relief. It was as if he had found who he was looking for. He walked over to us.

This man was purely luscious royal chocolate. Oh, my goodness he was fine. The closer he got to us, the finer he got.

Mmmmm. I moaned in my thoughts. *I could think of a few things he could help get jumped off tonight.*

Surprisingly, he walked right up in front of me and said, "Hey, I was looking for you, Lynn!"

Right then, I think my brain either melted or flat lined for a second or two because I was caught speechless. When I caught my composure, I softly and shyly asked, "Uh, you were?"

Then my friend rudely interrupted getting to the point. "Well, that's great because we need your help. Her car won't start. You know anything about cars?"

"Sure, what's going on with your ride?" he asked looking all helpful.

By this time, I was embarrassed three times. One, she yelled and screamed to call him over. Two, he saw my piece of shit car sitting there looking like something out of a nineteen sixty horror film. Three, her loud mouth, country ass was still talking shit with her potshot about *her car*. I was floored.

However, since he was sweet and accommodating and seemed to ignore all of the above, I decided to accept his helping hand that he so graciously offered.

"I had the car fixed yesterday and my shade tree mechanic told me I had to 'hit the wat-zik that was connected to my thingy stick with my shoe a few times' to get it to crank when it acted up on me." I repeated to him what the mechanic had told me earlier and he got under the hood and worked his magic in a flash.

"Wow! Thanks," was all I could say when his sexiness closed my hood, my car was cranked, and we were ready to go. I was so grateful and excited that I flung my arms around his neck and hugged him. "Thank you so much for all of your help!"

Unexpectedly, he hugged me back, but not like a stranger helping another stranger hug. He placed his arms around the grove just above my hip line and smashed my body into his hard body. I pulled back a little to look into his eyes. Damn, that man was sexy.

Just when we were about to make a truly subliminal

connection, Jessica pushed me aside and got all up on him. She rubbed his chest and while looking dreamily into his eyes said, "Yeah, we sure are grateful."

He took a step back, sized the both of us up, and then licked his lips. With the both of us bedazzled by his presence, he bravely made a suggestion.

"How about you two ladies get in the car and pull around to the back of the club and meet me there?"

On the inside, I was freaking out. This man was not just any star. He was one of the most famous dancers in the Chi, but as sexy as he was I didn't know about meeting him in no back alley.

He must have sensed my ambivalence because instead of us meeting him around back, he jumped into my front seat.

Even though she didn't drive to the club, Jessica jumped into the driver's seat, and I nervously jumped into the back seat of my own damn car. She had jumped her trifling ass in the driver's seat before I could say "yay or nay" to his offer. He seemed a little thrown off by the fact that Jessica was taking the lead and I was sitting silently on the backseat of my own car.

After she parked the car, they exchanged some small talk. I sat back there like a lump on a log listening to whatever I could make of their conversation. After a minute or two of chit chatting, her big dumbo head disappeared into his lap.

OOOUUUU, that nasty whore! What is she trying ta' do? She knew I was feeling him first, I thought as my skin began to boil. I turned my head away from the two of them and looked out of the window for a second. I swear could not stand Jessica sometimes. If I felt like a third wheel when they were talking, I surely felt like the fourth and fifth wheel now that she had her head in his lap. He looked back at me and pointing toward his lap whispering the words, "I wanted you."

I turned my nose up into the air as if the stench of his words were the foulest thing I'd ever smelled.

I whispered back, "Oh no! You've got the right one. She's much better at that kind of stuff than I am."

Yeah, my best friend was better at putting her head in a Negro's lap within the first thirty minutes of meeting him, even though said Negro was checking her best friend out first.

He snickered a little at my response for a second or two and then kept his eyes on her head bobbing up and down. Getting a little bold, he stretched his arm back towards me.

I started to resist, but what the hell. Instead of catching feelings, I joined my girl in turning his sexy ass out. What is that saying, if you can't beat them, join them. Plus, their little interaction was making me hella horny.

When he caressed my thirty eight double Ds into his palm and then reached inside of my low cut top pulling out my right boob to massage it, I thought *oh my! What is really going on here?* My friend's head was in his lap and his hands were on my breast.

While my mind raced and pondered over the petty details, my pussy juices were flowing steadily and craving every moment of heat from his wandering hands. I found my voice of reason long enough to pull his hand out of my shirt and say matter of factly, "You need to pay attention to what is going on up there."

"Huh, oh excuse me," he smiled mischievously. I was relieved when he turned his attention to my friend, who looked to be putting in overtime on his lower half. My girl was deserving of his attention for the effort she was putting in.

Instead of enjoying it, he lifted her head up and said, "All right lil' mama, that's enough of that."

She tried to resist his rejection, saying, "Why you do that? You were just starting to taste good."

He pushed her away with a little force and repeated himself. "I said that's enough lil' mama." He zipped his pants and hopped his happy-go-lucky, fine ass in the back with me.

"Hu, hu, hu," I could feel my breathing quicken, but it felt like couldn't breathe. I wasn't supposed to be feeling the feelings I had after he jumped off the front seat with my best friend giving him a blow job just seconds ago, but my heart was in my throat. I knew he heard it beating and felt me shaking.

He caressed my face softly, saying, "I won't bite, unless you ask me to." He placed his big strong hand under my chin and kissed me softly on the lips. Leaning back on the seat, he looked deep into my eyes, stroked his dick, and moved his hips suggestively. He was giving me my very own private show in the back seat of my car, and all Jessica could do is pout and watch.

Then, he said softly, "It's your turn baby. Do it."

When I shook my head no, he almost seemed to beg me to do it in a sweet kind of way. "Come on, baby. All I can think about is those pretty lips wrapped around this dick. I've been wanting to get at you for a long time now. Please give me what I want."

At his admittance of wanting me, my thought's shifted back to when he was dancing inside to how he came outside of the club looking around as if he were looking for me and then to him helping to get my car cranked, but inevitably my thoughts went to my best friend's head in his lap. I don't know why I let that bother me. It wouldn't be the first time that we had a three-way sexual escapade.

As I watched him beg me to take him into blowjob ecstasy,

I figured the reason that I felt such a connection with him while he was dancing earlier that night was because he was feeling me too. Our energies were connecting and we both were turned on by each other. He might have been giving me the eye while he danced, but his bedroom eyes in the back of my car were about to send me into a frenzy.

First, he put my hand on his manhood and rubbed it up and down his long shaft. It was throbbing, almost as if it had nostrils and was breathing on its own. His manhood was so vividly alive it had a separate life of its own from his body. I tried to resist answering his call for me to conquer him, but it was calling me.

I swear, I heard it whisper and pleaded for me to "Suck me Lynn. Please, kiss me. Wrap your succulent lips around me and suck me until I cum in your pretty little mouth."

When I finally snapped out of my trance, I realized that it was him talking and not his dick. Then, the weirdest feeling came over me. I thought about all of the nights I had dreamed of doing just what he was asking and begging me to do to him. I thought of the three hundred and fifty woman still in that club who could only wish that they were in my position, especially Tanya, Tamara, Tee, and Brenda. It was then that I made the mistake of looking down at that lovey, smooth, warm, honey-brown dick of his that was now out of his pants. It was jerking, waving, and pleading ever so sweetly for me to grace it with my lovely skills right then and there. At that moment, I knew resistance was futile. I gave in. *Jessica, eat your heart out while your big sistah shows you how it is done.* I was about to show my girl how to completely hold a man's attention.

WOOOOOSAH! I - I just couldn't resist his big brown mouth-watering yummy, juicy, dick- dick-Dick! Hold your position and wait a minute. I've gotta do an interlude real quick like!

Ladies, if you feel me, you must stand up, raise your right hand and repeat after me. It's our new National Dick Sucking Anthem. Now, proudly and loudly repeat after me, and give it all you've got: DICK IS GOOD, ALL THE TIME! ALL THE TIME, DICK IS GOOD!

(Repeat until you cum)

Thank you, now carry on...

Without breaking eye contact, I leaned over slightly. Just before I kissed it hello and delivered a lizard quick lick, I summoned all the dick suckin' Goddesses for their full attention and assistance. Then, I worked my pretty pink lip-gloss covered lips and tongue down his shaft. Less than one minute into my tongue torment of flickering and teasing, his legs started to tremble and his fingernails dug into the lining of the roof of my car.

He released the first sounds of a whimper before whispering to me, "Ooouuu baby, yeah. Just like that!"

Then, he began to run his fingers through my hair as he moaned and bucked as his deliciously huge dick further and further down my throat. The further and deeper he went, the more he trembled and moaned. I enjoyed looking up at him periodically and watching him enjoy me, enjoy him. Not once did I gag, which would be one thing that I would teach him. Bring on the best of 'em, I never gag. I got you boo.

His rhythmic thrusts and moaning made me hotter and hotter by the second. I was so hot that I was in melting chocolate ecstasy. I took so much pleasure in pleasing him that I thought I was going to cum before he did. As he screamed out my name, his body started vibrating so much that I actually thought this hunk was gonna have a heart attack in the back seat of my car.

At first, I thought he was gonna cry because it was feeling so good, but then came my hard earned reward. His hot cum exploded in my mouth. This man came so hard and thick, it was as if it was the first time he had ever received good head. After he went completely limp, his head fell back toward the back window.

How in the hell could I have explained our situation to the police if they just happened to drive up?

Let's see, "Young lady, step out the car. Could you explain to us again, better yet, why don't you show me, how this man died?"

"Well, ya see officer, what had happen was..."

As I sat back and watched him slowly recover, he looked completely exhausted and I felt just like Tony the Tiger, GREAT!!!!!!!!!

I rubbed the hairs on his chest and teased him, "I've been told that I deserve an award for giving dynamic head, but damn, uh, bay-be, are you all-right?"

He tried to talk some smack, but couldn't. He closed his eyes and he held his hand up weakly as if to ask me to wait a second. He finally managed to say, "I thought you said you weren't good at this. Pull my pants up for me."

"Well, I wanted you to be the judge."

He slowly opened his eyes and just looked at me like I was from another planet. He shook his head from side to side an said, "All I can say is damn! Where's my shoe?"

"Here it is," I said, placing it back on his foot." I had almost forgotten that he kicked it off before he came.

"Damn girl, you fucked me up!"

"50 cent might have the magic stick, but I've got the magic lips," I said, giggling proudly, as if I were a teenager or some love suck girl.

Then he said, "Look, magic lips." He kissed my lips tugging at the bottom lip before he continued, "I'm still on the clock and I bet they have been searching the whole club for me since I left out looking for your hot tail, so I got to go, but I don't want this to be our last time getting together."

"That's cool," I said, licking my lips and smiling. I kissed him once more. "Mmmm, thanks for every *drop* of your time."

We both laughed and said our goodbyes. He then opened the door, got out, and fell against my car shaking his head, as if to clear his head and gain his composure. He straightened up and staggered back into the club.

I sat there laughing and reminiscing about what I had just done with his sexy chocolate ass for a few minutes before I realized Jessica was not in the car. Once my chocolate treat had gone inside the club, she came walking out of the club exit toward the car with her arms folded. She was obviously mad.

When she got in the car, I said, "Don't hate. You would have kicked me to the curb to get another taste of his sexy ass too, so it's all good."

She smiled, and said, "He was packing wasn't he?" and laughed and that was that. Everything was cool.

I have to say that this latest adventure of engine trouble was not one of my naughtiest fantasies, but it could rival with the best.

As Jessica drove to her house, I talked her ear off about the entire experience. I was still complete disbelief. After she got out of the car, I got in the driver's seat and drove home in a nearly dream state. I climbed into my bed and began to drift off into fairyland, all the while smiling, reminiscing, and cumming.

Damn, what a hell of a way to end the night. Just before I nodded off, I made sure I respectfully, thanked all the Dick Suckin' Fairies for all their help. I drifted off to sleep with a full tummy and a big ass satisfied grin on my happy, pretty, and pink lips.

Dick Delivery by Luscious Lynn

So about three days after our encounter in the back seat of my car, a few friends were over at my house and Tee gave me a plug for the same stripper's big party coming up in the next month. Since Mr. OUUUDAMN would not be performing again until that party next month, I wouldn't get to see him for four long weeks. I wondered if he had thought of me, or even remembered the incident in the backseat of my car. Well, I figured since the tickets usually sell out fast I had better buy mine that day.

"How do I find out who is selling the tickets," I started to ask Tee, but then I remembered that, for the right price, the dancers for this stripping company would come to your home and deliver the tickets, in person. I could just imagine Mr. OUUUDAMN, in all of his glorious fineness there in my home. So, you know I called him, right?

The line to the stripper agency rang twice and he answered, "Hello." I knew it was him because the voice was deep and familiar.

"Um, hello!" I said sounding chipper as if I was calling for a normal take out delivery rather than a stripper delivery.

"Is this Mr.OOOUUU Damn?" I said.

"Yes, it is. What's your pleasure?"

I smiled at his corny line, and said, "Hi, this is Lynn. I hope you remember me from the other night? I need you to personally deliver two tickets for your show next month."

"Uh, excuse me," he said sounding confused. "Is this the Lynn that had car trouble a couple of days ago, and I helped you out?"

"Yeah, it's me. The one and only! I'm flattered that remember me and the *help* you gave me!" I said suggestively, once again too chipper for my own good.

"Hell yeah, I remember you, with those magical, pretty, pink luscious lips." Without even a hint of hesitation, he said, "Ah look, give me your address and I'm on my way."

I gave him the address and joined my friends back in the living room. After I had excused myself to freshen up and check my appearance, I spent the next ten minutes chatting with my house guests that were over for a spa party.

Just as I was about to fluff the pillows on the love seat, he was knocking on my door. I looked at the clock in surprise. Only fifteen minutes had passed since I hung up the phone. *Man, he must have floored it to get here this fast,* I thought.

"Ladies, you all carry on with the party. I'm going to get the door and will be back in just a minute," I said before I excused myself from the room.

You better believe that when I did let him in the front door I immediately forgot about all of my other company. We exchanged a sincere hug. I went for my wallet to pay him for the tickets, but he changed the subject and asked, "Will you show me where your bathroom is? I really have to go."

He appeared to be in a tight, so I escorted him to the bathroom on the second floor. Just as I was about to turn around to give him some privacy, he snatched me inside with him, locked the door, and leaned backwards against the wall.

"I saw all of the cars in the yard, so I know you have company," he said as he started to rub his dick, reaching under my mini skirt with his free hand.

He seemed delighted that I was commando – Ms. No Panties – for the day. So delighted in that fact that he knelt down, separated my legs, and raised my skirt.

I held onto the shower curtain rod, as he buried his mouth and tongue into my pussy, slurping and lickin'. He separated my lips and gave full contact directly to my swollen clit, finger fucking me at the same time.

"Oh! My, my, my. Yes! Oh...my!" I said between moans.

He moved his finger deeper into me until he hit my G-spot. I soared, "Mmmm! Oh my God. Do that shit daddy." To my surprise, I was cumming and begging him to "fuck me now, quick!"

Doing as he was told, he jumped up, turned me around, bent me over, and placed my hands on the side of the tub. This famous, fine ass, big dick, good fucking stripper grabbed my hips with one hand, plunged his engorged dick inside of me, and used his free hand to massage my throbbing clit.

My head swirled from the aroma of his intoxicating Usher cologne. Flashbacks of him dancing at the club danced around in my mind as I enjoyed his rhythm. Then my concentration was broken by the sound of one of my girls knocking on the door.

"Is everything all right in there, Lynn?" Brenda asked sounding genuinely afraid that someone had broken into my house and was beating me down in my bathroom. Well, that was kind of true, but there was no break in.

The sound of my friend knocking at the door did not stop Mr. OUUUDAMN from stroking my pussy hard and rhythmic.

"I'm...I'm...coming...in...a...minute," I managed to say between long pauses where I was biting down on my tongue to keep quiet. I suddenly felt myself coming with a surge that started at my toes and worked its way up through my entire body.

She must have heard the sound of our skin clapping together and me moaning and telling him to stroke me harder, because I heard her say, "Oh, I guess you are doing pretty *good* in there. Carry on my sister."

And that we did. The sight of cum dripping down my legs must have gotten him even more excited than he was before, because he sped up his strokes ready to make me repeat my climax four more times.

"Yeah, Lynn, come all over this dick for me. Cum for me, Lynn. Oh, yeah, yeah, yeah."

Yeah, I did what I was told and each time that I came I collapsed onto the bathtub with him catching me and pulling me back against his throbbing dick for more.

With my last orgasm, I became completely limp. He sat me back against the closed toilet seat. Standing in front of me with his back against the wall, he waited patiently until I recuperated.

Then, he asked, "Can we do it one more time, Lynn? I haven't been able to think about anything except how good you made me feel in the back seat of your car. Please, come over here and take this dick one more time, girl."

I happily obliged, knowing that times like these came once in a lifetime. And once again, I was helplessly under his spell. I sat up toward the edge of the toilet seat, grabbed his hips, and buried my face in his crotch. It made my heart beat a little faster when he gasped and moaned as I took his big dick inside of my mouth. I softly moaned as I went to work, pressing it against my face, inhaling the very essence of it.

"Mmmmm," I moaned, teasing him with the idea of taking him in completely. "May I have it all please?" I asked seductively.

"Lady, this dick belongs to you. Do your thang, girl."

I proceeded to cover the head of his tight, hard, shiny, swollen, aching [and a whole lot of other adjectives] dick with my warm and eager mouth. When I looked up at him again, his sexy eyes had closed and he'd put his head back and started sucking in air through his teeth,

So caught up in the moment, he accidentally knocked everything off the back of the toilet. He grabbed my shoulders for support and then used the toilet bowl cover to support his weight as he stiffened and presented me with a delicious nectar that I savored drop by drop.

After he stopped jerking, he just said "DAMN GIRL!"

He picked up his pants that he discarded on the floor before our sexual mayhem began, reached into his pocket and pulled out the comp tickets. Before putting on his pants, he handed me two tickets, and said, "You and a friend get in free and you eat free at the catered dinner, as well."

I thanked him kindly and placed a few singles in his underwear for the road. I patted him on the butt cheek and sent him on his way.

Before my dick delivery boy left, he said "Lynn, baby, you got a muh-fucka weak at the knees. Damn girl, I think I love you."

Lynn Marie Jones, writing as Luscious Lynn, is a literary new comer with a new spin on erotica – the truth, nothing but the truth, and the whole truth. She is a proud Chicago Chatham native and single by choice mom of two grown children. A twenty-one-year sarcoidosis survivor and an ex-professional dancer and singer, Lynn began writing after recieving her first diary. Her very life has been very eclectic and colorful. By the way, Luscious Lynn is her alter ego when she was 20 yrs younger.

"I credit my mom, Elissa, for instilling confidence in me," Lynn says when speaking of her mother. She also thanks Oprah [her shero] for inspiring her to be smarter, and for saving and changing her life. She has started on a new career path where she dreams of one day working with her favorites in entertainment, such as Usher and Tyler Perry.

"Dreams come true when you believe."

Beijing Beauty
"Er Nai"
by
Naiomi Pitre

<u>East Meets West</u>

I sat at the square bar in the equally square-shaped Sex and Da City Club, located in the Houhai District of Beijing, China. My drink of choice was Beijing Beer (Beijing Pijiu), and I was drinking it like the locals do – warm. While pondering the cultural effect that Western television had on the goings on in Mainland China, I stared at the club's low-key sign outside. I turned and took in the two-story mural of Marilyn Monroe that loomed over the bartender's head. I shook my head. *Sex and Da City, indeed.*

I had chosen my outfit carefully before leaving my hotel suite to meander my way to this place. Tonight, I was sporting a snug-fitting, black cotton, crew neck Dolce & Gabana t-shirt with black D&G button-fly jeans and matching leather belt. My shoes were a pair of well-shined Barker Black Limited boots. I was so particular about my choice in clothing due to the fact that I was a forty-three year old man, but I didn't want to look like one in the club. You know what they say, "black don't crack," so I didn't think I would have a problem fitting in. I was relieved to note that most of the men in the bar were older professionals, so that was alright. At six foot two, I towered over many of the Japanese gentlemen who drank their poison here, which adequately stroked my aging ego. To be sure there was no confusion as to my intentions, I was sure to wear my platinum wedding band proudly.

What exactly were my intentions, after all? My illustrious career as an investment banker was finally coming to its long-awaited crescendo. This week was definitely the most important one of my professional life, and to have it happening here, in this foreign city of dreams, made it all too surreal. I'd had an impressive run up to this point. No one could say that I hadn't paid my dues. Having glided through the Carnegie-Mellon FAST program, and subsequently working as an analyst for Goldman Sachs for several years before branching out on my own, I had proven that I had what it takes to succeed in this business. Now, I was the majority owner of Harris, Dennis, and Blackmon, the region's most rapidly growing investment banking firm. We started out small, but if my mother taught me one thing growing up, it was that with hard work, anything is possible, even for a poor, awkward, black kid growing up in the heart of Brooklyn.

I was visiting Beijing to touch base with one of my most affluent clients, Mr. Ming Nan Cheng. He and I would be reviewing a major trade proposition, which would mean millions to be made virtually overnight for our company. It was a move that had been a long time coming, and I was eager to get the ball rolling on finalizing our deal. I was in this club biding my time while I waited to become the richest Black man in the history of my entire family tree.

As I nursed my drink, I couldn't help but notice as the delicately graceful woman sauntered confidently into the club.

I swallowed roughly as I watched her modest curves slide back and forth, commanding attention, in the clingy, flame-red, satin dress. The sheath ended scandalously at her mid-thigh, with mischievous slits teasing me on both sides. Flirty golden sequins adorned the high-necked Mandarin collar, lighting up her heart-shaped, angelic face. She carried a small red clutch bag embroidered with more gold sequins and red ostrich feathers. Her hair was long, bone straight, jet-black, and layered. She wore it cascading loosely down her back.

My eyes followed her as she traveled purposefully up the stairs to the loft, where the tables called for a high price. She sat alone, her back very straight, glancing casually about the room while ordering her first beverage of the night.

I watched her boldly, never taking my eyes off the exquisite creature. It was as if she had entranced me. If only I had known then how her alluring sensuality would doom me in the end, maybe I wouldn't have let my emotions carry me on further. Maybe I could have left well-enough alone, and we all would have been happier, living lives they were familiar with, growing old in a mundane, but peaceful existence. It was ironic how, at this pivotal moment in my career, I would end up making such a detrimental decision.

As it was, her mysterious beauty had captivated me from the moment I laid eyes upon her. Perhaps it was the Asian beer that cast the spell on my better judgment, because my desire to drink in her very being proved insatiable. I watched as would-be suitors approached her table only to be smiled at and politely dismissed, one by one. Each time she would send them away, I smiled to myself, loving her decisiveness. If she had been more welcoming to any of them, I believe my interest would have waned. She was a forbidden Chinese treasure, not so easily claimed.

As I sat there studying her, another woman approached me, sliding her hand across my back suggestively. I immediately took her for a call girl, working the club, looking for some well-to-do businessman looking to part with his morals and his money.

"You like Beijing? You want to dance?" She asked, with a thick Chinese accent. She wore heavy foundation on her face, making her look more like a Japanese geisha girl, and her eyes were weighed down with far too much eyeliner swept up and out to the side of her face. I had the urge to grab a wet bar towel and wipe her face clean of the mask she wore.

"No, thank you." I answered with a smile, not unlike the polite expression the object of my attention was doling out to her admirers up above me.

"Okay. You change mind, you call me, okay?" She made a mock phone of her thumb and pinky, and with one last flirtatious rub, she was gone.

I leaned into the bartender and got his attention. He rushed over and leaned into me, to be sure he could hear me over the loud music blaring from the speakers. *In This Club* was playing, and the women were feverishly dancing to the hip hop flavor of Usher.

"I would like to send a bottle of Wuliangye up to the lady. Do you have any of the drum-type Old Liquor available?"

"Oh, that is very expensive, sir. A whole bottle? The lady is alone." He shouted over the bass-filled groove.

"I'm aware of the price. Do you have it?"

"Yes. We have." He nodded. "Whole thing? For one lady?"

"Give her the bottle, and tell her that it is from the man with the rose." I laid the necessary RMB down on the bar to pay for my order.

"Rose?" Confused, he called after me, as I strolled to the door.

I walked down the street, immediately hearing the aggressive touts of, "Lady Bar!! Lady Bar! You like to go to Lady Bar? Lady Bar!!"

I ignored these eager salesmen and admired the neon lighting and traditional red lanterns that lit the boardwalk. Vendors sold t-shirts and other wares all along the path, and I saw an occasional rickshaw driver speeding by, his day passengers having abandoned this popular form of transportation once the night had fallen. I continued to walk until I found a vendor selling an assortment of flowers on the sidewalk. I stopped and bought a single rose.

Taking my time getting back to the bar, I stopped to take in the beautiful scenery. I admired the Houhai Lake to the west, stalling as long as I could stand it before returning to my seat at the square-shaped bar in the center of the club. I forced myself not to let my eyes wander up to the loft. Now was not the time to catch her gaze. I wanted her to watch me for a change. I placed the rose in front of me on the bar and ordered another Beijing Beer. The bartender winked at me and nodded, gesturing knowingly at the rose. I didn't acknowledge his wink, on the off chance that I was now the object of the case study being conducted upstairs.

"That rose for me?" Another enchantingly gorgeous young woman approached me, just as I saw the Tammy Faye Baker minion from earlier climb on top of the bar and straddle one of the long silver poles on either side of it. She began to gyrate sexily along with the music.

"No, I'm sorry. It's not." I said, maintaining a charming smile. I was positive that I could feel the woman-in-red's eyes boring into me, but I still did not give her the satisfaction of acknowledging her. I stood from my stool and faced the new distraction. "Do you want one?"

"Yes. I want this one." She was wearing a yellow mini-skirt and a black halter top. Her modern black patent leather heels accentuated her calves nicely. I made a point of letting my eyes roam slowly over her assets. She grabbed the rose and placed it under her nose, sniffing deeply. "Smell nice...! What's your name, Mister?"

"My name? Why don't you tell me yours first?" I gently took the rose from her and laid it back on the bar in front of me.

"You can call me Tammy."

I laughed. "Tammy, eh?"

"Yes. I like that name. It's pretty." She giggled, reaching for the rose again.

I nodded, laying my hand on hers before she could grab it. "Okay, Tammy. I'm sorry. This rose is for my friend. She wouldn't be very happy if I gave it to you, I'm afraid."

"Oh." Pouting her full painted lips, she held her head down and looked up at me with those fantastically almond-shaped eyes.

"It's okay. I'm sure someone else will give you a rose soon enough. You are very beautiful." I leaned in to her to say the last part of my sentence, and she giggled again, as if I had tickled her. I was a connoisseur of inapproachable women, and I knew that in order to woo their hearts, they had to feel as if you were as in-demand as they were. I made my moves deliberately, playing the chess game of seduction like a professional.

"Thank you! Okay. Bye-bye." She skipped off to join her cluster of friends, and they cackled like a group of school girls.

Having yet to look up at my lady-in-red, I asked the bartender what I owed him. I stood up as I began to reconcile my bill, sure that I had gotten her full attention at this point. I knew she was wondering why I hadn't followed up on my advances. I took out a pen and jotted some information down quickly on my napkin.

"Are you joining the lady?" The bartender asked curiously.

"No. But give this to her if, and only if, she asks you about me when I leave. Tell her that it is from the man with the rose, and that I will see her soon." I made an obvious move to hand him the napkin, a move that could easily be seen from many yards away. He read what I had written and smiled, appreciating my suave American tactics. "Only if she asks you about me. Promise me?"

"Yes. You are... what do they call it? The Mack!" The man winked at me again and gave me a thumbs up. I smiled back, picked up the rose, and headed out into the night.

Having returned to my hotel and settled into the plush recliner in the main receiving room of the suite, I poured myself a glass of rice wine, and tried to relax. I was halfway through the bottle and also halfway to dreamland when I heard a confident rapping on my door. Smiling to myself, I walked over to the end table and retrieved the rose before answering the knock.

There she was, a satin-draped vision. She peered out from underneath long, sensual eyelashes, batting them at me curiously. Holding my napkin in her petite hand, she said nothing, simply gazing up at me.

"For you." I whispered, handing her the rose she had come all this way to claim. She held it to her nose appreciatively, never taking her eyes off of mine. "Please, come in."

The woman-in-red made her way over to the loveseat and laid elegantly across it, her dress riding up slightly as she did so. I made no attempt to hide my admiration of her toned and gleaming legs.

"Why did you wish for me to meet you here, American?" She spoke with the faintest of accents, her English very well-practiced. It threw me off for a moment. I wasn't expecting her to be so articulate.

"My name is Darnell. Darnell Harris. And yours?" I sat across from her, taking my place in my recliner once again. I leaned forward, getting a new glass and pouring her a cup of rice wine.

"Jinghua Peijing. Can you say that, Darnell Harris? Jinghua?" She took the glass from me and sipped slowly.

"Jinghua," I pronounced perfectly, "That is very beautiful. It fits you."

"Mmm..." She nodded, eyeing me.

We sat quietly, looking at one another, while we enjoyed our libations.

"Darnell, I noticed you in the club. I realize that you were watching me." Jinghua finally broke the silence. She had finished her wine, and set her glass on the coffee table. Laying back on the pillows of the loveseat, she draped her legs over one of its arms. "Do you mind if I take off my shoes?"

"No. Go right ahead."

I watched as she slid one foot over the other, her siren-red heels falling to the carpeted floor. Her feet were bare, save for the matching toenail polish that decorated her tiny digits. Jinghua's relaxed actions were in contrast to the fact that she hadn't even rewarded me with the slightest smile since entering my room. This leant a mysterious air to her presence that had a familiar effect on my nether regions.

"Yes. I watched you. You are a remarkable woman." I swallowed hard.

"Then why did you not approach me, Darnell Harris?" She asked in a sing-song voice. She was toying with me.

"Please, just Darnell. I watched you denying man after man at the club. I didn't want to be another one that you rejected without a second glance."

"How did you know I would not still reject you?"

"You are a woman who enjoys intrigue. You like a challenge. A mystery." I licked my lips, watching as she stretched her arms above her head, arching her back like a feline on my couch.

"Mmm... Perhaps." She turned her lithe body towards me and stared into my eyes. "I would like to fuck you, Darnell."

Jinghua's lips were on fire. They left scalding trails along my chest, down my stomach. Her fingertips were small flames, scorching my flesh wherever they landed. She straddled me, wearing only a cherry-red thong and garter set, her breasts free and standing at attention, each tan-colored nipple saluting me like a pair of tiny Chinese soldiers. She demonstrated her contortionist abilities, flipping around to straddle me backwards, arching her back to kiss me upside down before raising back up again.

I couldn't breathe. Her sexuality engulfed me. Her hair flowed down her slender back, tickling my stomach as she did an arousing dance in my lap. She leaned forward, rubbing my feet and my legs, and I watched her thong stretch up the crack of her behind. She leaned forward even more, and I saw that the panties were lodged between the folds of her completely shaven pussy lips.

Reaching forward, I rubbed her bottom with the palms of my hands, savoring the soft, silky skin. Not being able to contain myself, I laid a solid smack on one cheek, and the playful squeal she emitted caused my erection to jump. I used my fingers to pull up on her thong, watching as the undies split her tender sashimi in two. She moaned as I pulled up on them tighter, using my other hand to rub on the lips of her pretty pussy on either side of the panties. She arched her back while leaning forward, letting me fuck her with her underwear. I had wedged them so far into her that she dripped honey on either side of them, wetting my kinky pubic hair beneath her.

"Oh, Darnell, put your fingers inside of me. Let me feel you." She moaned, grabbing the bottoms of my feet and pulling herself forward. I was so turned on by a woman who would display her nakedness so boldly to me. Vivian was still a shy woman, despite being my wife of eleven years. She required that the lights were turned off, and that she keep an item of clothing on at all times (usually a negligee or silk teddy that could cover her belly). When I would accidentally catch my wife taking a shower, she would always make a point of draping a towel over the door so that I could not see all of her at once.

Yet here I was, this fantastically gorgeous woman leaning forward in front of me with the bedroom lamp light on, showing me all that Buddha had blessed her with. I sucked on my pointer finger, getting it damp with spit. Testing her willingness to comply, I rubbed my slick finger down the crack of her behind, next to the thong. She moaned heavily, continuing to arch her back. I took it as encouragement, slipping just the tip of my finger into her tight, puckered asshole.

She let out the most sensual scream, and backed herself into my finger. Before I realized what had happened, my whole finger was lodged inside of her. If she would have been able to see my face at that moment, she may have laughed at the shock that had registered there. My wife had *never* let me touch her in this area. Every time I had made any moves to do so, she would warn me away and ask me not to "ruin the mood".

I turned my hand so that my palm was facing upward and made a "come here" motion with the finger that was up her ass. She bucked wildly, shouting, "Ohh, yesssss... Darnell... You fuck me with that finger! You fuck me...!"

I used my other hand to pull her pussy lips apart by pulling at her upper thighs and buttocks so that she was showing me all she had. I took my finger from her tight crevice and pushed at her hips to indicate that she should turn around. I wanted to see her face and those incredible little breasts of hers.

This was another dramatic difference between my wife and Jinghua. Jinghua was a petite woman, with small perky breasts. Barely a handful. I had always enjoyed my wife's voluptuous body, with her size 44DD breasts, thick thighs, and ample bottom. This was a completely new experience. I had never made love to a slender or petite woman before. I wasn't sure if I preferred it to making love to my wife, but I was enjoying the newness of it. I had also never made love to a woman who was not African-American before, despite the taunts and teasing I had received in college about talking like a 'white boy'. I'd always been naturally drawn to my Black sisters. Jinghua's pale, but tanned, skin was a new frontier for me, as well.

She spun around with so much energy that just watching her revitalized me. Seeing her panties jammed into her from this angle was even more exciting. She rubbed herself on my manhood over and over, backwards and forwards, causing a friction that nearly blew my mind. Jinghua clutched at her own breasts, smashing them against each other. I reached out and tugged at her large nipples. She had big, thick nipples, but fairly small areola. I leaned forward and took one of those succulent meatballs into my mouth and sucked hungrily at it. She leaned forward to help me, her ass popping up in the air. I wrapped my arms around her, cupping her buttocks in each of my hands and spreading them apart, pushing them together, spreading them apart. Her nipple was heaven in my mouth, her skin hot to the touch. I let go of it, and grabbed at her, flipping her over to lie on her back.

"Will you fuck me now, Darnell? Can you fuck me like a good American? You sexy, American Black man!" She cooed, her full lips curling up at the ends to tease me.

I growled low and deep in my throat, ripping her thong from her little body. She giggled. I bent down and dove in for her intoxicating well, lapping up her hot sake with my thick tongue. Her clit was much more prominent than Vivian's, probably because my wife had a fat pussy with large lips and a bulging vulva. I grasped onto it with my lips, then grazed it softly with my teeth. She bucked and writhed underneath me as I tortured her mercilessly. My hands slid underneath her ass, and I lifted her sweetness to my mouth. I shoved her treasure into my face as my tongue thrusted in and out of her. She was sweet and tangy like eel sauce, and I savored every drop. For one silly moment, I laughed inside of my own mind, remembering something a colleague of mine had said in passing one day.

"Well, I would tap that from the side. You know why, right? Chinese women's pussies are all sideways... you know, slanted, like their eyes." I had laughed in spite of my usual reservations towards insensitive racist and sexist remarks like that, especially coming from one of the top analysts in our firm, but it sounded so ridiculous stated with his usual perfect diction. He said it as if it was a common phrase, like I should have heard it a million times before, like it was an old familiar joke, but it was the first time hearing the vulgar humor for me. And now I could tell him, although I never would, that he was wrong.

I reached over to my pants that had been discarded at the end of the bed. In the pocket, I dug out a silver wrapped Magnum condom and tore at the package with my teeth. Struggling to put it on my massive hard-on, I stared eagerly at Jinghua, who was arching her back for me on the bed, playing with herself in anticipation. It had been so long since I had used a condom that I wasted precious moments trying to get it rolled on correctly. When it was finally on, I placed myself above her tiny frame and hesitated.

"Oh, don't stop, Darnell. Come inside me right now. I need you inside of me right now." She pleaded, looking up at me with desire clouding her eyes.

For one fleeting moment, while I looked down on my Asian princess, I thought of my family back in the States. I thought about what Vivian must be doing right now, tucking in our twin sons, reading them a bed time story. I consciously brought to my recollection the day I spoke my wedding vows to my radiant wife, promising to be there for her forever under the eyes of a watchful God. My cock began to lose its power, and I could feel the condom growing loose. There was still time to turn away, to stop this madness right now, and ask God for forgiveness.

As if reading my mind and intuiting the encouragement that I needed, Jinghua started speaking in rapid Chinese. She reached up, grabbed me by the back of my neck, pulled me down to her, and whispered those foreign words deep into my ear. I had no idea what she was saying, but I could only imagine the nasty commands she must be giving me. She was working herself up into a frenzy, and I grabbed the base of my shaft, squeezing myself back to life. I pushed all guilty thoughts to the back of my mind and plunged myself deep into her central cavity.

As soon as she felt the initial penetration, she gave a long, low sigh, as if she had been waiting for this moment her whole life. I put my engine in overdrive, hammering into her like there were no tomorrow. She matched me, stroke for stroke, and we pleasured each other endlessly. I found myself wondering how such a little woman could take so much dick. Had she been with many other Mandingo warriors like me? I shook the thought away, burying it under the pile with my guilt.

Jinghua paused to flip herself over, getting on her hands and knees. I began to enter her doggy-style, but she shook her head wildly, caught up in the moment.

"No, Darnell. I want you to go where your finger led the way earlier."

For a second, I was confused. Then I remembered when she was on top of me in the reverse cowboy, and I had shoved my finger in her ass. I smiled, nodding to myself. This was a special moment in my life. No one had ever let me go into that forbidden territory before. I had tried several times, with several women, but not one of them had agreed. Vivian got angry every time I even mentioned the subject of anal sex.

"Are you sure, Jinghua?" I used my left hand to maintain my hard-on, stroking myself over and over. I used my right hand to rub her pussy juices into the crack of her behind. She was soaking wet, and there was plenty of natural lubrication.

"Hurry up, Darnell. You fuck me in my ass, right now." She whined.

I did as I was told.

Damn, this woman is gonna have me worse than pussy whipped. I'm gonna be Asian Ass Whipped! I thought crazily as the sensations shooting up my shaft threw me into overdrive.

Within seconds, I had slid my full ten inches into her snug love tunnel. Her rectum cling to my cock like the seaweed on the outside of a dynamite sushi roll. I felt every ridge and muscle squeezing the life from me. Her labored gasps sounded like she was loving her torture, and she grunted passionately with every push I made into the slim cushioning of her rearend. I could feel my peak coming, and I tried to hold back with every thing in me.

"Oh shit, baby, I'm cumming!" I bellowed, gripping her around her waist.

"Give it to me in my ass, Darnell. Feed my ass."

Her nasty mouth put me over the edge, as I felt my seed burst from my body, pouring itself into her asshole. It seemed as if I came and came and came until every ounce of my manhood had been milked from me. I collapsed on top of her, and she rolled out from underneath me, draping one leg over my back. She cuddled with me until I fell into a deep, satisfied slumber. Right before drifting off, I wrapped an arm around her small frame and whispered, "Don't you go nowhere. You'd *better* be here when I wake up."

"I don't plan on leaving you," she whispered back.

For the next seven days, while I was in Beijing conferring with Mr. Cheng, Jinghua stayed in my hotel room. We only left the suite to purchase new clothing for her to change into and to go out to eat whenever we tired of room service. The ease of falling into this type of pattern, as if we were a normal couple living in Beijing, surprised me. Walking hand in hand in the street, kissing passionately in foreign alleyways, and collapsing into one another's arms in our hotel suite each evening brought me back to the days when Vivian and I were first courting. I felt young again. I felt alive.

I couldn't believe my good fortune. Mr. Cheng informed me that he had decided to go with my firm long ago, and that the meetings here in Beijing were just to get me accommodated to the area and the culture so that I could better service him. After a long, very relaxed luncheon with Mr. Cheng and some of his closest colleagues, I returned back to the room floating on cloud nine.

"Darnell! You are home!" Jinghua rushed into my arms as soon as I stepped into the suite, just as she did every day. Planting several kisses all over my face, she pressed the length of her body against me.

"You always say that as if you didn't expect me to return," I laughed, slapping her across her behind playfully. "Give me a second."

"Sure, my love." She strode over to the mini-bar and began fixing me a drink. Her face was lit with the brightest smile as she gazed at me lovingly.

I sat on the loveseat and pulled out my cell phone. I punched in the first number in my speed dial memory.

"Hello?" An angel's voice answered.

"Hey, Mama." I grinned, excited to hear Vivian's voice across the ocean.

"Baby!" she exclaimed. It sounded like the kitchen sink was running. She turned off the faucet, and I could picture her drying her hands on our cream-colored dishtowels with the strawberries embroidered on them. "Are you off work already?"

"Yeah, Mama, this thing is in the bag. Mr. Cheng confided in me that he's made his decision already. It's a go."

I listened happily as my wife squealed, and I could tell she was jumping up and down. I chuckled, then looked over at Jinghua, who was staring at me with a bland expression that I could not read.

"Anyway," I shrugged at Jinghua questioningly, and she knocked back the drink she had prepared for me in one gulp. My eyes widened. "Everything's going great. I should be home in a couple of days, after I tie up a few loose ends."

Jinghua looked as though her pet puppy had just been slaughtered. Silent tears poured down her face, and she ran into the bathroom, closing the door behind her.

"Oh, wonderful, baby! The kids are waiting for you. They miss you."

"Oh, yeah? Just the kids, huh?" I teased, my mind in two places at once.

"Yeah." She teased right back.

"Hmmm...maybe I should stay out here a little longer, then." I stood, walking over to the bathroom door and opening it a crack. Jinghua sat on the edge of the claw foot bathtub, dabbing her eyes with tissue. She didn't look up at me.

"You'd better not." Vivian sighed. "I have to get back to cooking dinner, baby. You take care of my husband."

"Alright. You watch out for my wife."

"I love you, Darnell. Congratulations, baby. You deserve this."

"We deserve this. I love you too, Mama." I pushed the End button on the phone, double-checked that the call had been disconnected, then looked down at Jinghua.

"Babygirl, what's the matter?"

"What do you mean?" She rolled her reddened eyes at me. "You are kidding, right?"

"You've never had a problem with me phoning home before."

"Well, I never knew you were leaving in a couple of days, either. And you didn't tell me the good news about Mr. Cheng. You ran in here to call her and tell her first." She blew her nose, looking up at me accusingly.

"Jinghua..." I began to warn her, my voice growing agitated.

"What, Darnell? Do I not have feelings, too? I am just your little Chinese doll? Take me down off the shelf to play with me, put me back in my place when you don't need me, forget me on the shelf when you are done?"

"You knew as well as I did that my stay here would be brief..."

"... yes, but I thought that you would give me some warning before you..."

"And of course I would call my wife to tell her about my business success. She is the woman who takes care of my finances, my household, and my children. Why wouldn't I phone her to tell her about..."

"... I knew that you would, but why couldn't you tell me, too?" She continued to interrupt me.

"Jinghua..." I sighed. This woman was catching serious feelings for me, and that was dangerous territory. Having an international affair was one thing, a casual fling that my wife need not ever know about – making a woman fall in love with me and perhaps go *a-la-stalker*, that was another all together.

"Fine. It's time for me to leave, then. Let me get my things." Jinghua stood and pushed past me into the main receiving room.

I didn't make an effort to stop her. I only said, "You don't need to do that right now. We have a couple more days."

She spun around to look at me. Her facial expression transitioned smoothly from angry, to hurt, to almost hopeful. That part I didn't understand, until she spoke again.

"I have an idea."

When I broached the subject with Mr. Cheng the next day, he gave me a wide, knowing smile. I was relieved. I had envisioned him looking disgusted and telling me that he didn't want to have anything to do with me and my awful American misconceptions of his people. I had taken a big risk in mentioning Jinghua's suggestion to him, but at her insistence that it was a social norm here in Beijing, I made the jump. If it would have gone the wrong way, I would have been furious – at myself as much as at her. Risking my livelihood for a piece of ass, as exotic and amazing as that ass might be, was just ridiculous. To my relief, instead of scolding me, he laughed deep in his belly, leaning forward conspiratorially in his desk chair.

We were in the privacy of his inner office, and I sat across from him and his massive mahogany executive desk.

"You ask me of the 'er nai' tradition, Darnell?" Mr. Cheng's toothy grin put me at ease. "Something besides the food has whet your appetite here in this wonderful city, I see?"

"Well, you do have wonderful tastes to tempt the most discriminate of pallets, Mr. Cheng." I spoke cryptically, right along with him.

"The 'er nai' are very proud women. The elders called them 'concubines'. Women who were very happy to play their part in society. Women who did not even long to be a man's 'first wife'. Why would they? The first wife, although having all of the prestige of being the most important woman, the woman who would bear the man's sons, also has all of the problems. The first wife must cook, clean, mend clothing, and care for the entire household. She must bear the man's children and care for them sufficiently. It is her main priority to keep the man's affairs in working order. The 'er nai' is the second, or sometimes even the third, wife.

"She need only take care of the man's most primitive needs." Mr. Cheng winked at me. "She is to be very beautiful. A woman who helps the man 'save face'. She attends important functions with the man, and he gets the benefit of showing off a young, vivacious woman on his arm. He takes care of her. He buys her expensive clothing, feeds her only the finest foods, gives her an exquisite place to lay her sensitive head. She knows her place. She knows that she is not to be his most treasured, however she will be very well taken care of. To find a woman like this, whom you enjoy as much as she enjoys you, is very good fortune. No one expects a man to attend important functions with his first wife. Who is watching the children? The richest and most prestigious businessmen in China *all* have claimed their er nai long ago." The implications of his last statement were not lost on me. Mr. Cheng was a very well-established businessman in Beijing. He was not new to this concept in the least.

"Mr. Cheng. How would an American man go about having an 'er nai'?" I asked, intrigued.

"He would move to Beijing."

"That is not possible." I said, shocked by his answer.

Mr. Cheng guffawed, holding his stomach while he chuckled loudly at his own joke. "I am joking with you, Darnell. I have told you before. I like you. I like you more so now, knowing that you have acquired such a sought after treasure, having been in our fair city for such a short time. This is to be respected. Because I like you, I will help you."

He told me that there were several companies that he owned indirectly in the United States that could be used as covers to transport potential er nai's to the United States. They would be admitted into the country under a J-1 Exchange Visitor Visa, which would allow them to stay in the States as long as they were working as trainees for an American company. Once the company discontinued their employment, they would get their visa revoked, and INS would give them thirty days to get their affairs in order before returning back to China.

"It would be very simple for one of these companies to hire a woman from Beijing and allow her to live in the United States for as long as was desired by her... sponsor, shall we say?" Mr. Cheng raised an eyebrow at me. My heart leapt, then skipped a beat.

This man was telling me that I could actually bring my little China doll back with me to America? It gave me a feeling of great joy as well as filled me with tense trepidation. I couldn't risk being caught by Vivian. I had far too much to lose, and only a portion of it financial. Despite my recent actions, I loved my family dearly, and would never want to hurt my wife in that way. She had never done anything but be supportive of me and help me to grow the empire that was my business. Vivian had her faults, but overall, she had been an ideal wife. An ideal 'first wife'.

I pondered the fact that the Chinese people had come up with a perfect solution to the usual trials that a long-married couple encountered. A less than satisfying sex life, a boring marriage, the fact that a wife tends to gain a bit of weight and accrue a couple of wrinkles here and there with time – all of these problems were solved with an 'er nai'. The love for the first wife never faltered, but the er nai was there to supplement the man's needs. American women would never have the sensibilities to allow such an arrangement to exist, would they? On the other hand, I thought about all of the millionaires of the world and their kept women, the young ladies that they supported on the side while keeping up a public face with their wives. Was it all that different?

Thinking about the amount of money I was about to make, and what opportunities that would open up to me, I convinced myself that I could sufficiently sequester Jinghua far enough away from Vivian where she would never know the difference. What a stupid mistake that was. It would end up being the defining moment for the rest of my married life.

I nodded slowly at Mr. Cheng. "How long would it take to arrange the visa?"

"Six months. I will have my associate, Mr. Yi Xin, arrange everything for you. Give me her details and contact information, and after we leave this room today, do not speak of this to me again. If you have questions on the matter, address them all through Yi Xin. I am sure you can appreciate the value of discretion in this matter. If you mention this to me again, I will act as if I have no idea what you are speaking of. Here is his business card."

It was settled. The plan was being set in motion. I just hoped I could keep up with it once it was in full swing. I had no idea.

Back To The Daily Grind

"Hello, husband," Vivian said.

I stood up and smiled back at her, "Hello, wife."

The sound of small feet hitting the ceramic tile warned me that my twin sons were on their way to join the welcoming party. Bradley and Bryce came rushing at me from their playroom, throwing themselves at my legs. They were only eighteen months old, so I easily picked them both up, one in each arm, and hugged them tight.

"Daddy?!" The question and awe in their voices broke my heart. Had I been away that long? "Daddy?! Daddy home!"

"Yes, boys, Daddy's home." I laughed, squeezing them closer as they giggled in my arms. I finally let them down and watched them run off, the excitement having worn off for them just that quick. I shook my head happily. Those boys needed a hair cut. That was a duty I loved – bringing my boys into the local barber shop, letting them feel the camaraderie of the brothers, listening to everyone compliment me on how good looking my sons were. I'd make an appointment for the next week.

"Did you save anything for me?" Vivian sighed, pushing her bottom lip out in a sexy pout.

"You know I did." I rushed to her, careful not to step on Pearl and Onyx as I did so. I embraced my wife, kissing her deeply, letting her feel how much I had missed her.

"Whew...! What was all of that?" She laughed, backing away from me.

"I missed my wife."

"Wow. Well, I missed you, too, baby." Vivian started towards the kitchen. I used the opportunity to pat her on that plump derriere I knew so well. "I've got some pots cooking on the stove that I need to get back to. Why don't you bring those bags into the bedroom and take a quick shower. By the time you finish, I'll have dinner on the table."

"It smells nice, Mama." I picked up my luggage and brought them into our room. Taking her advice, I ran a steaming hot shower and washed the "travel dirt" off. While the steam drifted up around me, I let my mind wander back to my secret affair in China. I wondered what Jinghua was doing right now. I knew that she was a student in Beijing, staying in the small dormitory provided by the University. She was anxious to get away from the school and make her way to the States to follow me. Now that I was back home, I couldn't seem to reconcile this life with the one I had left in China. While I was there, the freedom and newness of being with someone totally different than I had every been with before, the ease of knowing that I would probably never get caught so far away, it had me resting in a false sense of comfort. Knowing that Jinghua would be here in Nevada in six months still unnerved me.

As much as it bothered me to think about what would ever happen if Vivian were to find out that I had not only met someone in China, had wild sex with her for almost two weeks, but also arranged to bring her home with me and start taking care of her here, it also excited me just as much to imagine being able to delight in Jinghua's sexual prowess and her uninhibited passion at my leisure. The water cascaded down my dark skin, giving me plenty of moisture to manipulate my sex.

I gripped my shaft at the base, letting the water run over my raging hard on. Picturing Jinghua swallowing all of my thick, creamy ejaculation, sucking all of the flavor from my taut sugarcane, I began to run my right hand down my cock at a fevered pace. Even better, remembering how she had begged me to cum all over her face and breasts, insisting that it was the sexiest thing about a man, being able to make her feel so dirty, I swiped forcibly at the tip of my mushroom cap with my thumb.

Vivian never swallowed, saying that her gag reflex would always kick in no matter how hard she tried. Whenever I had even mentioned performing a facial on her as an alternative, she would wrinkled up her face and call me *nasty*. Her words had discouraged me from suggesting anything far from the norm with her. I knew that she wasn't open to experimentation in the least. But because I respected her, loved her intelligence, desired her bountiful body, grew prouder of her educational accomplishments day by day, and remained in complete awe over her exceptional mothering abilities, I never once had the urge to cheat on her before Jinghua. No woman I had ever met since I had been married could hold a candle to her in my eyes.

Visions of Jinghua bouncing enthusiastically on my cock ran their course through my mind, and jacking myself into oblivion, I felt my eyes cloud over with that familiar feeling of losing oneself at the brink of release. I squeezed my eyes tight, then opened them quickly to watch my seeds get washed down the drain. I finished washing up, rinsing off, and stepped out of the shower to dry my body.

Throwing on a clean pair of boxers, some basketball shorts, and a black t-shirt, I headed out to sit at my dinner table with my family. The clan had already gathered, and my boys couldn't keep from staring at me with huge Kool-Aid grins. I wondered if this was how soldiers felt when they returned home from leave, as if their children didn't quite know what to make of them. Trying desperately to step back into your normal life and stop being a stranger in your own home.

The dogs had no problem remembering me. They sat at my feet, each one taking their post, lying on their stomachs, with their head and forepaws covering one of my feet on either side of me. This warmed me through and through.

Vivian had truly outdone herself. I looked across the table as she brought in the last bowl, a heaping mound of sweet corn. My favorite dishes lined our table, including twice-baked macaroni, marshmallow candied yams, smothered pork chops, collared greens cooked with bacon, cornbread pudding, and fried catfish.

"Who's going to eat all of this, Viv?" I laughed. She finally sat opposite me at the other end of the table, grinning sheepishly.

"I haven't had to cook like this in two weeks. The boys just wanted fish sticks and hamburgers." My wife was proud of herself, and rightly so. As we ate, joked, and played with my sons, I savored the moment. This was what life was about. This was living. This was exactly what I had worked so hard my whole life for. Why I would soon put all of that in jeopardy, I couldn't have answered in a million years.

That night, I laid on my back with my arm around Vivian. Her head was nestled snuggly on my chest, her fingers playing in the light bit of fuzz on my stomach. We were so comfortable in one another's arms. I knew she was expecting to have sex on my first night back, but I almost just wanted to lie there, smelling the sweet vanilla body mist she wore, relishing in the faint left over smell of her jasmine-scented shampoo. I kissed the top of her head as she let her hand roam further below, to the elastic waistband of my boxers. My breathing came rapidly, anticipating my wife giving me the ultimate welcome home gift.

Without saying a word, Vivian lifted herself up on her elbow, bringing her face down to my belly to plant soft kisses there. I sighed inwardly. I knew this meant that she wasn't in the mood for giving head tonight. Whenever she would hesitate and spend a lot of time kissing me above my pelvis, I knew that was all I would get that night.

I took the hint and got up, pulling my boxers down quickly. Like a well-rehearsed play, we each performed our own choreographed steps. She rolled over onto her back. I stepped to our nightstand and turned the lamp off for her. Getting back in bed, I lifted her long satin nightgown, but just to the top of her underwear, no further. She lay quietly, looking up at me with love seeping from every pore of her curvaceous body. I slipped her underwear down her thighs and off the ends of her well-kept feet, pausing just for a moment to tickle her playfully. She giggled, then stifled it, as if afraid to speak or express herself too loudly in these intimate moments.

I silently pleaded with her to talk dirty to me. I screamed out in my mind for her to go down on me like a champ, savoring every drop of my salty man-juice like it was her only life line. I struggled internally, begging her to just let go and let God make this marriage exciting, make our sex incredible.

Instead, I climbed on top of her, riding her sexy body like a wave. Her sweet sex was like a moist pillow, and I rested in it. I gave her all of me, and she showed off her skilled internal Kegel muscle control, pulling and compressing me within her. This quiet bit of naughtiness was her one offering up to me, and I grasped at it like it was the last bit I would have to eat for forty days and forty nights.

When I came, I came inside her, knowing that because of her surgery after the birth of our sons, we were in no danger of having any more children. I didn't think about whether or not Jinghua would have given me some type of sexual disease that I could be potentially giving my wife at that very moment. Whenever anyone ever speaks about cheating, that is one of the first questions women will inevitably ask. Honestly, I didn't give it a second thought.

We fell asleep spooning on our sides - me resting behind her ample bottom, cupping her breast with my hand, she gripping the top of that hand with all she had within her. Holding on to our lives together, holding on to our strong marriage, putting the love we had shared for the last eleven years in a vice grip so tight that my hand eventually went numb just before I nodded off.

In the middle of the night, I awakened abruptly. I realized that I had made a grave mistake. My heart began to thud within my chest, and I slid my arm slowly from Vivian. Stopping in the bathroom to rinse and drain my dick, I entered the bedroom again, kneeling to pick up my boxer shorts and pull them on. When I looked up from my task, Vivian was sitting straight up in bed watching me.

"What's wrong? Where are you going?' She held the covers close to her, like a little kid, clutching them as if she had had a bad nightmare.

I strode over to her side of the bed and reassured her with a loving kiss to her forehead. "Nothing, baby. I have some unfinished business to attend to. You had me all hot and bothered, I forgot all about it."

Vivian was quiet, searching my eyes with hers.

"You better not be asleep when I come back upstairs. I might want round two." I tried to alleviate the awkwardness.

"Back upstairs? You going to your office?" I didn't understand the quiver in her voice. She knew that I often worked at all hours of the night due to my dealings in other countries with different time zones.

"Yes, Mama. You just keep it warm for me, okay?" I smiled and extricated myself from the room, pulling the door closed behind me. I stood on the other side of it, in the dark hallway, until I heard the soft sounds of the bedsprings as she laid back down. I made my way downstairs, and across thirty-five hundred square feet, to the opposite side of the house. We had this home built specifically to give me privacy away from the usual bustle of family activities; it boasted an office that was insulated for sound and had a locked door for privacy from snooping little toddler eyes and sticky fingers.

I crept into the office now, locking the door securely behind me and walking across the large room to my writer's desk. Turning on the computer screen, just in case Vivian had followed me downstairs, I picked up my private office phone line and dialed a number far, far away.

"You forgot about me." This was how she answered the phone on the first ring, as though she had been sitting beside it all this time, since I had first left her side.

"Never." I sat back in my ergonomic chair and rested my feet on my desk.

"Hmph..." Jinghua snorted, then switched gears. "I miss you so much, Darnell!"

"Me too, babygirl." I smiled, running a hand across my smooth, bald head.

"Six months is far too long to wait. My pussy is yelling for you right now. Can you hear it?" I heard rustling sounds and gasped as I realized what she was doing.

"Did you just rub your pussy with the phone?"

"I stuck my phone *in* my pussy. It still doesn't match up to you. But it smells nice now."

I shook my head in disbelief, laughing uncontrollably. Soon, she joined in.

"I know; six months is too long. But it is up to Mr. Cheng now. He has said that he can't speed up the process any more than that. I'm sorry, babygirl."

"But what am I supposed to do while I wait? I am so bored here, waiting to be with you. Nothing makes me happy anymore." I could hear the pout in her voice. It melted my heart.

"I'm going to send you something to make you feel better, okay?" Picturing the look on her face when she received the gown that I planned on purchasing for her from N.E. Tiger, the most exclusive and fashionable designer in Beijing, I smiled at myself. The outfit she had worn the first night we met was probably from the same designer.

"You will?" She sounded happier already.

"Yes. And tomorrow morning, I am opening a private account at the bank, in just my name only, until you get here, so that Vivian doesn't know about the money there. I will be doing a wire transfer to your account number that you gave me. You will just need to call me with the Swift Code, so that the bank can get it easily." I spoke quickly, my mind racing a mile a minute.

I knew that tomorrow morning I was expecting a large sum of money from Mr. Cheng for some of his ventures, and I planned to have it wired into my new account. There was a personal banker at the branch closest to my house that would always flirt with me when I made a stop through there. Normally, because of the large dollar amounts in our accounts, we were assigned to a private banker in the corporate office downtown, but ever since I happened on the cute sister who worked locally, I tried to stop in every so often to let her stroke my ego a bit. I knew that she could be counted on to be discreet and not ask too many questions.

"You would do that for me, Darnell?" Jinghua sighed, happily. I grinned.

"You know it, babygirl."

"Okay. Swift Code, right? They will understand what that is?"

"Yes, they know what I mean. Your account number tells my bank which account to send the money to, but the International Swift Code tells my bank which bank in China to send it to. Call me on this line, because no one enters this room when I'm not here. It remains locked, and I am the only one with the key. It's my office. Leave a message with the code as soon as possible, okay?"

"Okay. And you said you are sending me a surprise, too?" She giggled.

"Yes."

"No present could compare to having you right here beside me, petting my pretty little pussy... But, what is it?" Like a kid at Christmas, she questioned me.

I loved her naughty nature. The mischievous grin remained plastered on my face. "You'll see, babygirl. Now, let me go. I will talk to you soon."

"Wait! Darnell?"

"I'm here."

"Was the first wife happy to see you home?" She murmured.

"The 'first wife'?" I was taken aback by her use of this strange term. It felt odd coming off my lips.

"Yes. Your Vivian." Vivian's name sounded even stranger to me coming from Jinghua's mouth. I didn't like it. I wanted to snatch it back out of the air and make her swallow it again as if it had never been uttered.

"Uh, yeah... the first wife was very happy." I vowed that I would always refer to her this way when speaking to Jinghua, and I wouldn't allow Jinghua to do anything different. That would be the last time she said my wife's name.

A pause. "Okay."

"I promised you. I will take care of you. You don't need to worry about anything any more, okay?" I said, softly.

"Yes, Darnell. I believe you." She paused again. "I will believe you if you learn three words for me."

"Okay. But you know I'm no good at the Chinese dialect."

"Say 'wo ai nee'. Repeat it after me. 'Wo... ai... nee'." She pronounced it slowly.

I tried.

"Very good!" I could hear her clapping gleefully.

"What does it mean?"

"It means 'I love you'."

Now the pause was mine.

"Wo ai nee, Darnell." Jinghua tried.

"Wo ai nee." I hung up and rubbed at my temples.

My cell phone rang while I was at home five and a half months later.

I had spent the last five months sending Jinghua expensive gifts and wiring thousands of dollars to her. I didn't think Vivian expected anything, since none of our finances suffered, and the money I was using to finance my new "business investment" was new money, coming from sources she wasn't in the know about.

My nights were divided amongst quality time with my family and being holed up, 'taking care of business and loose ends' in my back office. Jinghua and I had been partaking in the joys of long-distance telephone sex, and with her knack of utilizing her filthy American vocabulary skills, it definitely was quite enjoyable on my part. She had fucked me six ways from Sunday countless times, using nothing as her tools but my imagination and past recollections.

When my cell phone rang, I was sitting on the couch in our family room, watching a DVD that Vivian and the boys had picked up on the way home from a dentist visit earlier that afternoon. I thought nothing of it as I glanced at the phone, saw it was a number from Beijing, and pushed the Talk button. I knew that Jinghua only called me on my office line, and calls from Beijing to my cell phone were always legitimate business contacts.

"This is Darnell Harris, of Harris, Dennis, and Blackmon Investments. How may I help you?" I spouted off by habit.

Vivian was laying her head in my lap, her feet propped up on the arm of the couch on the other end. The boys sat on the carpet, underneath us, focused wholly on the movie playing on our big screen plasma television.

"Mr. Harris. My name is Yi Xin." The man's voice was thick and heavy, completely no-nonsense. Briefly, I had to try and run through my mental rolodex to place the name.

"I'm sorry, Mr... Xin, was it?" I struggled to stall him and remember why I should recognize the name.

"Yes. Mr. Cheng has asked me to contact you in regards to a Ms. Jinghua Peijing of Beijing, China."

I sat up straight, nearly knocking Vivian off of me. She was startled, raising up to look at me, concerned. The boys turned around to stare at me, as well. I tried to recompose myself, casually laughing off the incident. I pointed at the phone and mouthed to my wife, *I gotta take this.* She nodded, having no reason to question me.

"Yes, Mr. Xin! Very good to hear from you. All the way from Beijing, is it? Great! And how is our partner, Mr. Cheng?" I raised my eyebrows at Vivian and smiled, heading towards my office. Once there, I locked my door and sat at my desk, secure in the fact that the room was nearly soundproof with all of the extra insulation.

"We would like you to know that a package will be delivered to your place of business tomorrow morning. Inside, you will find all of the details regarding Ms. Peijing's safe arrival to your country at the beginning of November. You will have her flight number and all of the necessary details. The company that she is training with in the United States will be listed, along with her supervisor. She will be training as a home consultant, and will not be required to come into the office to work. However, as the package will explain to you, to keep all paperwork in order, Ms. Peijing will need to report to her supervisor once a week to sign a log that will be available to any government official who may need to request proof of her employment."

"Okay. That sounds great." I had only spoken to Mr. Xin once before, almost four months ago, when he called just to introduce himself and tell me that he would phone me once the arrangements were closer at hand. Now I recalled how business-like he conducted himself, and could see why Mr. Cheng had chosen him to deal with such delicate matters.

"If you should have any questions once receiving your documents, please do not hesitate to phone me." He rattled off a number which I quickly programmed into my phone. "Otherwise, Ms. Peijing will arrive at the designated airport at the designated time, and she will expect to be picked up accordingly by either yourself or your agent."

"Oh, I will pick her up." I responded, a little too eagerly.

There was a brief moment of silence.

"Yes. Thank you. Very well then." And just like that, he was gone, like the Wizard of Oz, giving me my wish and poof! Disappearing in a puff of smoke behind the curtain.

I couldn't wipe the grin from my face. The day had finally come.

Chapter Three – Fantasies Fulfilled

I knew that she was angry. Her heels clacked menacingly on the concrete, telling me so. I carried her bags through the airport garage purposefully, attempting to avoid a loud public confrontation. She stalked three or four steps behind me, huffing and puffing the whole way.

I felt more than a little guilty. I knew exactly why she was salty with me. When I saw Jinghua step down the escalator towards baggage claim, my heart leapt up into my throat. I couldn't breathe. She was as gorgeous and as glowing with energy as ever. But when she screamed out to the top of her lungs and charged at me, her arms thrown wide in the air for an embrace, I cringed.

There were too many people in this area. Everyone stopped what they were doing to glance back at this extraordinarily beautiful woman, who would get looks if she never did one thing to call attention to herself, and to see who she was so eager to meet up with. That was dangerous for me. My wife had lots of friends and acquaintances. She knew a lot of people in this city. I diverted my eyes, looking away and walking towards the carousel where her bags were located.

She continued to call out, catching up with me and grabbing my shoulder, oblivious to the hints I was throwing her way.

"Darnell!!!!" She hugged me intensely, crushing me against her bosom.

"Jinghua." I hugged her at a distance, holding her away from me and patting her back like an over-excited auntie. She looked at me, puzzled. I kissed her cheek and turned towards the carousel once again. People had finally stopped looking by now. "Let's go get your bags."

"Uhm... okay." She pouted.

Now, walking towards my car, she acted like a spoiled child who hadn't gotten her way. I knew that she must be thinking that this was the way I would be here in America, that this was what I had brought her all the way here for. I tried to think up a way to make it up to her.

It turned out that I didn't have to. Once we reached the vehicle, it was as if she had forgotten how to be angry. I pushed the key alarm and unlocked my trunk to put her bags inside.

"Oh my gosh!!!! Darnell!!!! Is this your car?!" She squealed.

"Yeah." I smirked, tossing her bags one by one into the compartment before closing it securely and looking up at her. She clutched her hands together at her chest, blinking rapidly as she gave the car a once over.

"But this is a 2009 Porsche Cayenne Turbo S!"

I looked at her, amazed, with one eyebrow cocked in the air. "How on earth do you know that?"

She laughed, running her hand lightly over the hood, careful not to mess up the gleaming shine. "Porsche held their premiere of this beautiful car at the auto show in Beijing this year! A few girlfriends and I were modeling for the show. I was lucky enough to model this one. This is the Lava Gray Metallic color, isn't it?"

I chuckled, shaking my head her way. "Wow. Yeah. It is. It's exclusive to this years Turbo S. Get in the car, woman. You continue to amaze me. Not too many people know their vehicles like that."

"But how did you ever get this vehicle in the first place?" She pressed on, as she slid into the buttery leather seat, feeling it automatically heat up while I maneuvered the car out of the narrow lanes of the garage.

"Excuse me?" I tensed. Far too many people wondered the same thing, here in Las Vegas, when they saw a Black man driving this type of vehicle. They wondered the same thing when I moved into their nice white neighborhoods, too. It was a sore spot with me, and I wasn't about to let her question me like that, along with every one else I'd ever had to justify myself to. Too many people with too many assumptions that a man like me should not be able to afford such luxury had me quick to jump on the defensive. Her light skin made it even easier to do so. "What is that supposed to mean? You know what I do for a living."

"I *mean* that it is November, and this car only debuted in August in the US. It sold out within the first two weeks of production! People are on a waiting list for years to get a car as customized as this one is." She pushed the button to open the sunroof, looking like she was in a daze.

I wasn't too big to laugh at my own foolishness. I patted her on her tight exposed thigh. "Oh, well, babygirl, you know that I have my ways. They had to sellout to somebody, didn't they? Someone had to buy that car within the first two weeks, right?"

Jinghua took the first opportunity, at a red light, to lean over and throw her tongue down my throat like she had originally wanted to in the airport. We quickly got lost in one another's embrace, causing the cars behind us to start blowing their horns when the light changed without our noticing.

We came off the I-215 Beltway, into the suburb of Henderson, Nevada. It was the furthest I could get from Summerlin and Vivian. We lived on the northwest side of town, and Henderson was about the furthest southeast that you could go and still be near the city proper.

The condo I had rented for Jinghua was fully furnished. It was perfectly located directly across from The District, Henderson's most exclusive shopping area, which boasted quaint boutiques and many fine eateries. Within a ten mile radius, Jinghua would have access to the Green Valley Resort, Spa, and Casino, with its movie theatres, pampering spa facilties, and hot nightclub. In the other direction was Liberty Pointe, which offered indoor and outdoor aquatic centers, an outdoor amphitheatre, basketball courts, parks, and more!

Jinghua's face was alight with wonder and amazement as she took in the level of luxury and decadence with which her condominium had been laid out. We made love in every possible room within the next two hours.

"You have spoiled me, Darnell." She laid naked in my arms, draped haphazardly across the floor of her spacious walk-in closet and dressing room.

"Only because you deserve it, babygirl. I am so happy that you are here, finally, with me – where you belong." I let the moment sweep me away. I ran a light hand over her breast, tracing my finger around her right nipple.

"I am so deliriously happy. I can't believe how lucky I am," she sighed.

I lift up slowly, gazing into her lovely face for a long while before standing up.

She immediately looked sad. "Darnell, we need to discuss something very important."

"Okay."

She stood up to face me.

"Darnell, what you did tonight in the airport was not acceptable."

I laughed without meaning to. She looked so serious, and she had placed her tiny hands on either side of her slim, naked hips. Looking like an x-rated oriental Brat doll, it was hard for me to take her seriously. Jinghua glared at me, and I straightened my face, nodding at her with a serious expression.

"I'm serious!" She whined.

"I know, babygirl. I'm sorry. You just look so damn cute." I wrapped my arms around her and held her tight. She let me hold her, melting into me, but then pulled away.

"Seriously. Now, I know what it was about. I'm not dense."

"There were a lot of people in the airport, Jinghua. My first wife..."

"I know. But what you have to understand is that in my country, one of the best things about being an er nai is that you are the showpiece. You are the woman that the man is *proud* to be seen with in public. I should be your ornament. Your jewelry. Or... like your Porshe!" She smiled, happy with her own metaphor. I listened intently, trying not to smile again. I knew she was being serious.

"Okay. Fair enough. But we have to be careful."

"Right. Now, I forgive you for the airport, because I was a bit too excited. But from now on, when we are around this area... you did say that this area is very far from your home, or where first wife spends her time, right?" Jinghua continued.

"Yes. As far away as possible."

"Then, as long as we are here – in this home, and around it – we do not hide. You show me off. We have fun. Just like in Beijing." She waited for my consent, smiling up at me, craning her neck due to her short stature.

I thought about it. Didn't see the harm. Vivian didn't know anyone in Henderson, and she rarely did any shopping or recreation outside of our neighborhood. She didn't have to, because Summerlin was a lot like Henderson. All encompassing. We had everything we needed with a ten to twenty mile radius of our home, just like Jinghua.

"Okay. You're right. I want to show you off. You'll be my trophy."

This made her very happy. She reached up and gave me the sweetest kiss.

"I have to get going now. I can't have the first wife starting to question things right off the bat. We need to keep this as unsuspect as possible, when we can."

"Okay..."   She performs her signature pout, and once again, I'm like a snowcone in the middle of July.

"I have something for you."

I go out into the living room, and she follows close behind. Pulling open a desk drawer, I hand her a small box.

"What...?"

"These are your checks. There are two check books in here. I have signed all of them, but I have left them blank."

She looked at me in awe. Her mouth gaped open. "H-h-how much?" Jinghua stammered.

"If you need more than ten thousand in one month, you need to call this number and let me know. I can have it transferred quickly. For now, my name is the only one on the account. I needed you here with your identification, to sign onto the account. We'll do that this week, but for now, you call this number."

"What is this number? Your office phone? I have it."

"No, now that you are here, you may need to contact me quickly. What if I am not in my office? This is a special cellphone that I purchased just for you to contact me. It's pre-paid, under someone who works in my office's name, so no loose bills or ways to trace it to me."

"Ooh... okay." She still looked like she was in shock as she stared at the box in her hand, the small box that was worth thousands.

"This is the number to call while you are here. If I don't answer right away, just leave me a text message, and I will answer you very soon."

"While I am here? Are you planning on sending me away, Darnell?" She cocked her head to the side and looked at me pitifully. Tears welled up in her eyes.

"Of course not. You know I plan to keep you here as long as you like."

She smiled at me. Before I left, I made sure that she had been given all of the information that I had, regarding what she needed to do to report to her supervisor and stay legit.

"One last thing, babygirl."

"Yes, Darnell?"

"This." I dug in the same drawer and pulled out a set of keys. "Go to the condo parking garage. Up to section 3D. That's the third floor, section D. Press this button, and your car will beep at you. It's yours."

"Oh my gosh, Darnell!!! You bought me a car?!"

I laughed. I had leased a little used BMW for her to drive around town in. It was under the company name, and could be easily explained away, should any tickets or anything like that pop up unexpectedly.

By the time I left her condo, Jinghua was flying so high and so excited to rush to the garage that she barely noticed me leave. I'd have to admit that the feeling I received from spoiling her was addictive. Knowing that I had the know-how and the means to take care of a woman as fantastic as her while still maintaining a family life on the other side of town was an aphrodisiac. I was The Man, and no one could have told me otherwise. I had the er nai to prove it.

Returning home that night, I ate dinner with the family as usual. Vivian and I read the boys their respective bedtime stories and turned their night lights on. We headed off to our bedroom, and she turned to me just outside the door.

"I'll see you in a bit." She dismissed me flatly, and turned away.

"What do you mean?" I asked.

"Well, aren't you headed to your office to finish up?"

Had I been that regular about not sleeping with my wife? Had I been so preoccupied that this had become a nightly routine that I hadn't even noticed?

"No." I followed behind her, grasping her by her waist and letting her lead the way.

"No?" She seemed surprised, but didn't seem all that thrilled. Something wilted within me.

"What, I can't sleep with my wife?" I tried to make light of the situation.

"You tell me." She laid down on the bed and turned away from me, pulling the covers up tight around her body. I looked down at her and sighed.

Lying down myself, I turned the other way, towards the wall. With Jinghua's silky juices still drying on my cock, my lips, and my fingertips, I had enough to carry me through the night. I didn't have the energy to deal with her emotional breakdown right that minute. I let her have it.

Before I drifted off to dream dirty dreams filled with red dragons and square bars with stripper poles erupting from them, I barely overheard the sound of my wife sniffling beside me. Beside me, but so far away.

Chapter Four – What Is Done In The Dark

Vivian Harris puttered about her home, content in her daily tasks. Ever since she had the twins, she had quit her job as a mortgage broker, staying home to focus on raising her children. The timing had been perfect, as Darnell had opened his firm ten years before, and was beginning to bring home serious money. They could finally afford for her to be a housewife, something she had always craved as soon as she had fallen in love with Darnell and knew she wanted to have his children some day.

He had promised her that quitting would not be the end of her personal growth in any way, shape or form. Darnell wanted her to continue taking classes at University of Las Vegas, in any subject that she desired. He encouraged her to explore her own interests, get involved in the community, maybe even open her own business one day.

She enjoyed writing fiction, and that gave her tremendous pleasure. Due to her wide online presence, her author interviews and online magazine articles were very well known. Vivian toyed with the idea of opening her own bookstore one day and inviting out of state authors to conduct signings for local reading groups.

The University was where she had learned a lot of her culinary skills. She took several courses there, in art, Black history, creative writing, but the cooking classes were what got her going. She loved being able to throw down in the kitchen. It was the one room in the house that she dominated. Vivian knew that when she stepped foot in that kitchen and started burning pots, no one could deny that every dish she created was fierce. Her family loved her cooking, and her friends always praised her for it.

As successful as she was at creating heat in the kitchen, she would think it could translate over into a certain other room in the house, but it didn't. Vivian had begun to worry about Darnell. He would spend hours upon hours, after tucking in Bryce and Bradley, locked up in his office downstairs, leaving her to sleep alone in their cold, lonely bed.

She had done that night after night for two weeks when he had traveled to China that last time, and she had quickly found that she hated it.

But even after he had returned home, and even more so as of late, he was absent when she was ready to turn in for the night. She tried to dismiss it, knowing that she was definitely reaping the benefits of his hard work and dedication. If it weren't for the Beijing trip and Darnell's late night hours, they wouldn't be able to do half of the things that they were able to for the boys now. Darnell had also just bought her a commemorative anniversary wedding band for their twelfth year.

"This isn't one of the special ones, though." She remembered pointing out to him, when he had handed her the small ring box, and she had opened it to find the huge rock staring back at her.

"What? That thing cost me..."

"No, not the ring, silly!" She had hit him playfully upside the head. He was so quick to respond before someone finished their thought. "The anniversary. You know, not the tenth, or the fiftieth, or even the twentieth! This is far too special just for the twelfth!" Slipping the gorgeous platinum setting on her finger, she admired it at arms length.

"Every single year with you is special, Mama."

She loved when he called her Mama. He had only begun that pet name for her once she had bore his sons. Ever since, that was his term of endearment for her. It pulled at her heartstrings each time he uttered it.

Yes, she knew that she definitely reaped all of the benefits of his work, but that didn't stop her from missing the man she loved more than she'd ever known it was possible to love a man. The man who had given her two darling twin boys who looked like spitting images of him. The man who had shown her nothing but respect, never calling her out of her name, or raising a hand to her, in over a decade of marriage.

Sometimes she would play counselor to her female friends, and they would relay awful stories to her about things that their mates had done. Cheating with their relatives, slapping them around, trying to touch their daughters, and Vivian would be mortified. She always told them to respect themselves enough to demand it from the ones who claimed to love them. But Vivian knew that the only reason why she could sit on that high horse, stand on that soapbox, was the simple fact that she had gotten lucky with Darnell.

They had met young, while in high school, but they hadn't dated in the beginning. Her mother and his mother hadn't gotten along, having lived down the street from one another nearly all of their lives. Their long-running feud kept Darnell and Vivian away from one another for a long time.

As they grew older and went their separate ways, Vivian had decided not to attend college. Her mother didn't have the money to send her, anyway, and her younger brothers and sisters needed her help. Mama was always trying to make ends meet with several odd jobs, and once Vivian graduated, she had begun to work full-time, bringing home her paychecks to help out.

She had heard from friends that Darnell was going off to some fancy school in another state, on some fast track to becoming a banker of some sort. He eventually came back to New York to do an internship, and much to his mother's dismay, Vivian caught his eye once again when he saw her around the old neighborhood. Old flames die hard. At this point, Vivian's mother had heard the rumors about this young man who seemed to be on a shooting comet towards success, and she had no problems with her daughter grabbing the tail end of it and going along for the ride.

Vivian quickly fell smitten with Darnell's charm, good-looks, and quickly building success. They dated off and on, while he focused on his work and school, and she continued to help support her mother.

One day, twelve years ago, Darnell came and told her that he planned on moving across the country to Las Vegas. She was so excited for him., but so sad for herself. She knew that this meant saying goodbye. He wanted to open his own investment firm. He was finally going to make all of his dreams come true.

Little did she realize that those dreams included marrying her.

Of course, she accepted and followed him, wide-eyed and naïve, to the big city of Las Vegas. That was where he'd made her one of the happiest women in America.

As she reminisced, she went into the boy's rooms to check up on them. It was early afternoon, and they were each sleeping in their own beds. She had stayed in with them today instead of taking them on an outing to the park or to the library, because they had both come down with a cold. They had been running a fever last night, and she had given them medicine that had kept them groggy into the day.

Darnell was concerned the night before, but she was happy that he had all the confidence in the world in her abilities to take care of their children while he was gone. Her nurturing abilities were another trait that she was most proud of. It was like all of the practice she got taking care of her siblings growing up had paid off. Mothering came naturally to her.

The boys were deep in heavy sleep, and as she always had a habit of doing, she stared at them for a few seconds too long, holding her own breath while she watched their little chests to make sure they rose and fell like they were supposed to. She knew it was a silly superstition, but she was always worried about that their breathing would stop while they slept. She didn't want to think about that too long. What would she do without her boys, the ultimate joy in her life? No, she didn't want to linger on those thoughts for too long.

The house phone was ringing. She bet that it was Darnell calling to check up on them. Rushing to the kitchen, she picked up the receiver and said hello.

"Hello, is this Mrs. Harris?" A woman's voice asked her.

"Why, yes, it is. May I ask who is calling?"

"Yes, ma'am. This is Brenda Tackturn from your local Wells Fargo bank on Craid Road?"

Vivian thought for a moment. That wasn't the name of her banker downtown. Their private banker's name was...

"I'm sorry, Brenda, but we handle all of our finances through one of your private bankers. Mr. Jacob Winters, out of the downtown branch?" She figured it was a routine solicitation call and readied herself to hang up the phone.

"Yes, ma'am. I understand. However, I have been trying to get in contact with your husband, Mr. Harris? Darnell Harris? He was in my office a few weeks ago." Brenda spoke hesitantly.

"Oh." Vivian drew a blank. She knew that Darnell used the local branch's drive-thru window out of convenience at times, but she thought he did all of his business through Mr. Winters. They always had in the past. "Well, what was it that you needed? I can easily get in contact with him."

"Well, Mrs. Harris... it's just that the account that I am calling on is one that you are not a joint owner of, and so I am limited as to what I can tell you." Brenda cleared her throat.

"Well, then, Ms. Brenda, you are going to have to wait until my husband comes home around six this evening, and address him then." Vivian was getting a bit perturbed. She knew that Darnell had business accounts that she wasn't involved in, but this woman should have his office phone and cell if that was the case.

"The problem with that is that this situation is of the utmost importance, and it needs to be addressed as soon as possible. Uhm, it involves a high *overage*..." Brenda paused.

"Overage? I'm sorry, I'm not following you."

"A non-sufficient fund amount on the account that needs to be rectified as soon as possible. I have probably said to much already. It's just that I have been in close contact with Mr. Harris about this account, and I would hate to have the manager close down his account or enact the right-of-recourse action, which means paying the overage from one of your other accounts, without Mr. Harris or yourself being aware of it." Brenda had significantly lowered her voice at this point, as if she didn't want someone around her to overhear her conversation. "You see, Mrs. Harris, it involves a transaction that I used my authority to override, due to my relationship with your husband. He is a very good customer of mine, and a valued business client as well. I allowed one of his checks to go through and signed off on it, sure that he would deposit enough funds by the end of business day to cover the amount. Now that this large sum has bounced, it falls on me to rectify the situation."

Vivian heard the nervousness in the young woman's voice. She could imagine the woman's boss breathing down her neck to correct this mistake. There was a large boulder growing in the pit of Vivian's stomach.

"Brenda, if you want to rectify this situation, you will give me some details. I can be down there with cash within minutes. If you insist on waiting for my husband, he won't be able to call you until you open tomorrow morning, because when he gets home tonight, you will be closed." Vivian stated, matter-of-factly. There was a long silence while Brenda Tackturn decided on the better of two evils.

"Mrs. Harris, the reason why I am calling is because your husband's account is negative in the amount of seven thousand two hundred and fifty-six dollars and eighty-two cents."

Vivian drew in a quick breath.

"I overrode the check and let it go through, because he always keeps plenty of money in that account, and the check was written out to the co-owner listed on the account."

"The... co-owner? If there is a co-owner, why didn't you call Mr. Dennis or Mr. Blackmon to rectify it, then? I'm sure it was just an honest accounting mistake on their part. In doing their line of business, it would be easy to do. They are all business partners, and if you call the work phone listed, you're bound to reach them." She was relieved. It would be an easy fix. Hell, she would call one of them herself if she needed to. This young girl was overreacting. Seven thousand dollars probably represented a few months pay to her.

"Ma'am, the only number listed is this one and Mr. Harris' cell, which I have left numerous messages on. And this is a personal account, not a business one. The co-owner... I believe he said it was your adoptive daughter? A 'Ms. Jing-hoo-uh Pee-jing'? I'm sorry if I've mispronounced that."

Vivian paused. She swallowed. Her mouth remained dry. She swallowed again. "Is there a number for Ms. Pee-jing?"

"No, like I said, this is the only one. And like I said, I only overrode it because it was written from him to your daughter, which is not unusual for this account. He's written several checks greater than this one before, and even if the money is not immediately available, he's always gotten it wired before the end of the day. They've come in several times together in the past, so I didn't think anything was unusual. Unfortunately, this check was cashed yesterday, and nothing has been transferred yet."

They'd been in the bank together?

"Wait... there is another number! It's under 'alternative contact'. Would you like for me to call it instead?" Brenda nervously back-pedaled.

"No, it's probably just my cell phone number. What is it?"

As the banker recited an unfamiliar number, Vivian jotted it down on the notepad she kept next to the phone. "Yeah, that's my number." She lied.

"I'd really appreciate your help with this matter, Ms. Harris..."

"Missus Harris! Missus!!" Vivian shouted, her hand that held the phone shook uncontrollably.

"Oh..." Brenda paused, uncomfortably. "Yes, ma'am. Missus Harris."

"I'll see what I can do."

Vivian pressed END and replaced the cordless phone back on its charger. Staring at the once inanimate object that had suddenly morphed into a cold black messenger of doom, she attempted to weigh her options. Was she overreacting? Perhaps she was being silly. This 'Pee-jing girl' could be an associate of Darnell's at the office. His reasons for sharing an account with her could be completely legitimate. Because she probably wouldn't understand anyway, he didn't mention much about his dealings with the new Chinese account that had brought in so much money lately. If she went flying off the handle, it could jeopardize their relationship and also offend him that she hadn't had enough trust in him. That was the last thing that she wanted to do.

Aside from his long hours in his home office in the evening, Darnell had never given Vivian any reason to doubt his loyalty to her and their marriage. Even the long hours could be explained. This new Chinese account was allowing them to afford all of the best things in life, and far be it for her to complain about what he had to do to bring in the money that she had no problem spending.

Darnell had always treated her like a precious gem all his own, and she couldn't see him doing anything that would ultimately take him away from his home, his sons, and his comfortable lifestyle – especially not now, when everything was going so smoothly for them.

And yet, there was a nagging suspicion urging her on, tempting her to pick up the phone and dial the mysterious woman's number. After several minutes of looking from the quickly written numbers back to the phone, she wrenched it off of its cradle and made the call.

Her breathing increased, and she struggled to slow her heartbeat. She promised herself that she wouldn't say anything rash. She would give the woman the benefit of the doubt, assuming that she was a business associate of the firms. They would discuss the banking matter and hang up the phone like two civilized adults.

After four rings, Vivian heard the familiar click of an answering machine picking up. She nearly hung up the phone, until she heard the sexy voice on the other end giggle suggestively and finally speak.

"Hello, you have reached the home of Darnell and Jinghua Harris. We are not in at the moment, but if you would like to leave a message, please do so at the sound of the tone. Thank you so much. Zàijiàn, and goodbye!"

The clatter of the phone breaking into three pieces as it hit the ceramic tile was deafening, but it was lost on Vivian, who had landed right beside it in a dead faint.

Naiomi Pitre is a force to be reckoned with!

In her debut novel, BROKEN VOWS, an intense drama unfolds between a jealous husband who lacks self-esteem and a sexually explorative wife who craves a taste of the forbidden. Book clubs, reviewers, and readers alike are raving about this sizzling story! Naiomi's second book was released in 2007, IN THE PANTY DRAWER - Journey Into The Mind of a Sexual Woman, and quickly followed in the footsteps of BROKEN VOWS as a new favorite read! Pitre has also recently released a new steamy erotic poetry CD entitled HOW NASTY IS TOO NASTY.

Her most recent venture is starting her own press company that services authors and other business men and women seeking to create and market their products. For more information on Naiomi, go to her website at www.imoianpress.com

Other Titles from Nayberry Publications

Order Now at
www.nayberrypublications.com

7194795R0

Made in the USA
Charleston, SC
02 February 2011